Island Paradise

Also by Kathy Page

Back in the First Person
The Unborn Dreams of Clara Riley

KATHY PAGE

Island Paradise

Methuen

For D S and N B

I would like to acknowledge a debt to
Pacific Woman Speak, Why Haven't You Known?
published by Green Line, Oxford.

An earlier version of *The Lens*
was first published as work in progress
in *Writing Women Vol 4 No 3*.

First published in Great Britain 1989
by Methuen London
81 Fulham Road, London SW3 6RB

British Library Cataloguing in Publication Data

Page, Kathy, *1958–*
Island paradise.
I. Title
823'.914 [F]

ISBN 0 413 19690 9

Printed and bound in Great Britain by
Richard Clay Ltd, Bungay, Suffolk

Contents

We can speak of it as a revolution, sudden but bloodless, brought about by four very wise men who had the courage to answer their people's cries and follow where history led.

Teacher's notes on
Post-war History, year 23.

We have bowed our heads and turned away from slaughter. Wilfully Inflicted Untimely Death cannot but be absolutely forbidden. We shall henceforth for the first time adhere to natural prohibition.

Preface to
New Code of Law, year 1.

'The International Force is of course not a military force. Neither is it a peace-keeping force: it is a peace-making force, organized, for the sake of efficiency, rather as armies used to be. . . .'

Joint Commander Selburn,
International Force, Recruitment notes, year 36.

The Island

You're supposed to go for a medical when you're fifty, but I avoided mine. There are things I don't want seen, marks and blemishes no ordinary flesh could have acquired. Signs. And things I don't want to hear: 'Expect to be a little depressed as your life draws to a close. Visit Age Counselling if you need help. Try to establish a perspective. Eat less, sleep more. Let go . . .' *Let go* – I imagine my fingers holding on to the edge of a cliff, uncurling, one by one. And there are many things I don't want to let slip, because I had an adventure I shouldn't have had. For years both H and I have tried to forget what happened to us; we agreed at the end, or what we thought was the end. But while H seems somehow to have succeeded in his forgetting, I've failed. Night after night I've lain awake in our grey cool bedroom, rocked by waves, remembering that world of constant heat and vivid colour, danger, unexpected solace, loss.

It was twenty years ago, and exactly a hundred years since the Unfought War. Memories were slowly fading, as if, in a process the very opposite of photographic development, they had been swirled in a bath of warm liquid and dissolved like so much gelatine. We had been saved at the last minute of the last hour; we were grateful not to be dead. The bad stuff was over. We lived carefully, worked hard, appreciated the pleasures of daily life. We went on holidays, as many as we could. That's how it was, and how it still is: except I'm different.

For a start, I've nothing to do. No right, wrong, click! No totals at the end of the day, no pep talks, no congratulations. I'm not part of progress any more. That's how it is when you retire. One big holiday, but you can't go away. All day there's nothing, except wandering the streets talking to other old people, but because we're all scared to draw attention to ourselves or let on exactly how old we are, we don't do that. We stay in, trying to eat less, sleep more and establish a perspective. We are paying the Price. These are the kinds of things I should be telling an Age Counsellor, not myself, at night.

Back then, before, I went to work each day. Kim would wake me. We took a shower by preference. Kim's working day started a little later than mine. I dressed neatly, walked a couple of blocks, stopping on the way to catch the morning announcements. I was in the circuitry department of Components Inc. They've been bought and sold, subsumed and digested a few times since; I think they're part of General Manufacture now. I verified connection and resistance. Right, wrong, click. I chose this profession at school, because I seemed to have an aptitude for fine work, and I liked the teacher, Luna Parlow. A year or so later I chose Kim as my lover, because of the soft hair on the back of his neck and the hesitant way he took my hand; also because my mother had died, right on Time, followed weeks later by my father, and I think I felt a little lonely in the world; I was young.

If I'd worked harder, I could perhaps have designed circuits myself, but instead I examined someone else's patterns, some so small as to be absolutely invisible to the naked eye, magnified thousands of times on my screen. They were beautiful, intricate maps of something that couldn't be seen any other way. I would work steadily, and alone, through the appropriate schedule of tests – sometimes this would take several days – and at the end of it I knew the thing was perfect and would work or it was flawed and would not: I found this satisfying, day in, day out. Right, wrong, click. I think I was quite happy. After a couple of years they let me work at home, sending someone to visit me once a week. It was quiet work, safe, relatively free of stress, and of course there were no anxieties about the future: circuits are like skin cells, thousands die each day and have to be replaced.

The certainty of it all is what I remember: you tested things, you could do it for ever; it was useful, you were required for something outside yourself, going somewhere: progress, a great ship ploughing through soft clouds into clear sky. And, like everyone else, you would die when you were fifty-five, give or take a few years, women the same as men. In Time Before, it's said, we women used to live longer, and men used to hurt us. Now it's fair, and they don't. We all work. *Two nations have become as one.*

So: it was summer. I was going on holiday with Kim. He was working in Pesticide Development. 'There's a new bug born every hour,' he used to say cheerfully and slap his hands together as if extinguishing an imaginary fly or mosquito – in company this little joke often embarrassed me, seemed somehow obscene – 'I'm a busy man.' We'd been together more than five years but never taken oaths; there didn't seem much point. Although, as I said, I think I was happy then, there were times when I thought about the rest of life and it seemed impossible to imagine continuing so long, day in day out, right, wrong, click. Now and then I developed a slight tic in a muscle on my cheek and had to go for medication.

'I'm tired,' I'd say to Kim on such occasions and then burst into tears or drop something. 'We need a holiday,' he'd say. We went three or four times a year, just little breaks. But our trip to Island Paradise was something we'd saved for. Leisure development on the island was restricted, and so we had to book several years in advance.

The publicity promised huge vistas, sky and sea and sand; simplicity and, of course, peace. Excited, I held Kim's hand tightly in mine – though we were still at the airport, I pointed things out as if we were already somewhere else; I speculated endlessly, ran through the publicity time and time again – 'Do you think it can really be –?'

'Must be. Why say it otherwise –?'

We'd waited so long for this, and, as it happened, our departure had fallen on Anniversary Day. There was to be free champagne and in-flight entertainments. Soft music played as we embarked; the stewards handed us badges bearing the symbols of the rocket and the dove. *Dreams come true*, the publicity said (and perhaps, after all, they did. Or will: you have to give them time). We strapped ourselves in and lifted off; the weather would be fine, day in day out; we couldn't wait –

Kim and I lived together, as H and I do now, but then I had friends as well. Martina, for instance. Once a week, she and I used to go swimming. She was a big woman, effortlessly strong despite her sedentary life. Thick straight hair, the colour of dark chocolate but fiercely glistening, swung down to her hips. She wanted to have a child, but lacked both the proven years of relationship and the required joint income. Somehow they always fell just short. We swam up and down the lanes until we were tired and then we would go, glowing and loose-limbed, to sit in the dark of the planetarium, the pictures or a lightshow. We never went dancing or anything like that. After our swim, we liked to be still.

'Oh, I envy you, Laurie. Oh, I do,' she'd whisper as we watched, light flickering over our faces. 'I mean, I'm sick of Joel really. I should get myself someone else, one of these space boys – but then we'd have to start all over again, another five years . . .'

'One of you is bound to get a rise soon,' I'd mutter

soothingly. It was a kind of ritual, this whispered conversation; we never looked at each other as we spoke, but sometimes I could tell she was crying.

'The trouble is, it makes me *hate* him . . . oh, sorry . . . don't tell a soul, Laurie. . . . It's not his fault, and I know the rules are only fair, I wouldn't have it any other way, good god, I wouldn't – not how it used to be – but – I want to ask him to leave – if I did, he'd probably get a rise the next day – oh shit –'

I'd feel a little guilty, because I didn't care so much about what I had, and yet she wanted it so much.

'Why is it,' she'd ask tentatively, 'why don't you and Kim –?'

'I don't know,' I'd say. 'I just don't.' Part of it, I knew, was that you're stuck together once there are children. And somehow, despite the soft hairs on his neck, I didn't want to be stuck with Kim. At the same time, I couldn't imagine anything different. We used to arrive home within minutes of each other. We were on the third floor of a medium-sized Residential, bigger than this, backing on to the river. Dove City. We liked to cook, prepared our meals together, ate them looking at the water. We played games, watched shows on telescreen. At night we lay down quietly side by side, put on some music, and sometimes, always rarely but less and less as time went on, we'd make love, and there were times among these when I'd feel very afraid, of myself, for him, and draw away.

Martina would sigh, and shift in her seat.

'Sometimes I imagine what it'll be like if I never have one. . . . I imagine it feeling a bit empty. . . . I'd like to feel I'd given something to the future. That it wasn't just the end. . . . Sometimes that feels more important than anything else. . . . The future's more important than now, isn't it, somehow?'

'I know what you mean,' I'd say, glad to be on more general ground, 'that feeling of all the things outside of us we don't know about and can't touch. A pull, a kind of undertow . . .'

'My job doesn't help,' she'd add, nodding, 'seeing old people all the time. They say it's high stress. Mind you, we get the holiday to make up for it, but I haven't the money to go anywhere exciting . . . just the same old places, inland mostly, you know.'

Martina was in Age Counselling. I don't think I'd get on with her nowadays. If we had the same conversation today, I think I'd call her a hypocrite. I'd say: it's all part of the same Price, Martina dear; remember (as if, I think now, you could forget), peace doesn't come free, and safety isn't cheap. We won't die starving or suddenly and hurting, picked out by a sniper, squashed by a bomb or a badly designed vehicle hurtling down an ungated street, like they did in Time Before, but neither will we live to be a hundred and four and get a telegram from the president. And neither, Martina, can we have a baby just precisely when we want, any old how. A small Price to pay, in the small print of the Treaty that saved us all from ourselves, Martina? She must be getting old now, as well.

Martina used to make jokes about her clients, describe their mannerisms, their disintegration. *How can they live with it?* she used to say. *Disgusting*; some just won't *let go*. Most of them infuriated her, one way or another. The strength of her antipathy embarrassed me a little, but even so I didn't stop to think about it. I didn't imagine myself here, now; didn't think I would be one of those *hanging on*. I didn't think, as I do now, that what happens to us old contradicts every other clause and sentiment in the Treaty. You don't, on the whole, think about these things until you have to.

To cheer herself up, Martina told me, she hung stills of young people in her office: adolescents, close up; their unmarked skin, shadowless; their eyes fixed determinedly ahead: time to come. I saw Martina just the day before Kim and I left for Island Paradise. That was the last time. She gave me a squeeze.

'People say a holiday like that sets you at it like a pair

of kids,' she remarked, laughing. It was only when we sat together in the dark that she got so sad, about what she couldn't have. When I consider it, as calmly as I can, I do even still think it is a small Price to pay. So long, that is, as we get what we're paying for. Guaranteed.

We were cruising. The rumble of the engines was very subdued; all the noise was left behind us, but that faint and distant hum, that slightest of vibrations, seemed to fill me up entirely. I turned off the patterning game set into the back of the seat in front.

What are my dreams? I thought, and found my mind as blissfully blank as the shifting whiteness beyond the window at my side. What do I want? What would I have different? Nothing. Pure white.

'I'm happy,' I whispered to Kim, 'very happy.'

> *... Sleep under canvas or under the stars themselves if you wish, and pass the day on one of Island Paradise's beautiful shelldust beaches, listening to the slow sounds of the sea.... Hurry to book your place, because everyone wants to go to Island Paradise just once in a lifetime, just once....*

When I looked at Kim again, his eyes were shut. The lower part of his face had relaxed completely, his mouth was half open, his cheeks slack, but his forehead was as ever bunched into a tight frown, as if he was reading very small print in his sleep. I went alone to the bar cabin. It was empty and the bartender occupied building transparent pyramids with small plastic goblets. Without waiting for my order, he poured two glasses of sparkling wine, spilling much of it.

'Complimentsh,' he said.

I smiled and raised my glass. He held up a warning hand.

'No,' he said, 'Not "Happy Anniversary" and not "to Island Paradise" – save that for later.' He drained his glass immediately, and poured another. His face was young, but his hair, thick and unruly, was grey. If I had hair like that, I thought, I'd use some dye. In poor light you could be taken for old.

'Here we sit,' he continued, staring at me with a mixture of belligerence and melancholy, 'drinking Anniversary champagne – courtesy Holiday Flights Inc., about to feast our eyes on those emerald forests, those perfect beaches –' His gestures were sweeping and extravagant, his voice rose and fell, stretching the words out. He began another pyramid on the counter between us, setting the goblets down unerringly by touch alone, still not looking away from my face. He lowered his voice. 'Asking for trouble, don't you think, a name like that?' He giggled.

'Are you alright?' I asked. 'Shall I get help?'

'I'm fine. You're fine. You'll have a lovely time,' he said. The pyramid grew steadily. 'Don't mind me,' he said. 'I'm just drunk.'

I was almost frightened of him, and stood very still, smiling rather inanely.

'Help yourshelf.' He pushed the bottle of champagne towards me. I didn't take any.

'Do help yourself,' he articulated carefully. 'Must have something to celebrate. Haven't we all? Your dreams are coming true.'

'But I haven't got any,' I said. 'I was thinking before I came for a drink, I don't have any, I don't really know what it means. That's all right, isn't it?'

'All right? Of course. But I'm very surprised,' he said. 'Everyone has their dreams. Mark my words, I see them on their way back and they all look different. *Happy*'s the word they use –' He leaned towards me. 'D'you wanna be happy?' he asked, grabbing my arm. I felt I was supposed to say no, and pulled sharply away.

'I'm already happy,' I said. 'D'you give this performance to everyone you serve a drink to?'

'No, I'm not part of the show.' He dismantled the pyramid methodically, stacked the goblets, wiped the counter.

'You'd better go back,' he said softly, 'you'll be missing it all. Just drunk. Sorry. Sorry.'

I considered making a complaint about the service but, after all, I was on holiday and he had apologized. I slipped back beside Kim, waking him.

'Is there anything you'd have different?' I asked him.

'What d'you mean?' he said blearily. 'But no. Well, Laurie, you know I'd like us to have a child. We could; it seems a waste not to.'

My voice rose. 'I've told you all along I'm not the mother type, I don't want –'

'Sssh,' said the steward disapprovingly. 'Let's have no harsh words.' He bent over us to pull down the blind, turned off Kim's pattern. 'It's about to begin.'

We sat silent in semi-darkness, flying through dense cloud at approaching the speed of sound. The curtains drew back from the telescreen, which was blank but glittering, as if images were jostling behind it, preparing for resolution. We shuffled in our seats, fiddled with the headrests. Far behind us a small, weary voice protested, 'I want to look out of the window,' and was told, 'Stella, there's nothing to see. Only sky.'

What a name, I thought. Poor kid. That was the fashion then, classrooms were like constellations. We stared at the blank screen. I too felt restless. 'Nothing to see in here neither!' said Stella under her breath.

'I do know,' whispered Kim. He took a deep breath, his hand reached for mine. 'I'm sorry.' I took his hand. The steward smiled. Behind us, a small and ineffective, but distinct, slap, followed by a gasp. A shiver of disapproval passed through the nearby seats, quick glances were exchanged.

'Sorry!' said Stella, and her mother, almost simultaneously. 'Sorry, very sorry.' Stella sighed.

If your heart beats faster, that's what you say: sorry.

You say it as quickly as you can, you wrap it round like a bandage to staunch blood, or squirt it like foam on a fire; it's supposed to mend things, to make it as if they never happened. When I was a kid, sometimes I used to whisper another word in my head when I had to apologize: 'I'm –' (not) 'sorry.'

The lights dimmed and we were surrounded with music, full resplendent sound that moved always from the minor to the major keys, a slow crescendo of interlayered sounds, each drawn to a focus like rays of light to a lens. I felt myself relax, grow warm and expansive. I'd always found music comforting. As a child I had learned to play notes like these on a keyboard of my own. I'd blended pure sounds layer upon layer until the end, when I would see in my mind's eye images of departure: rolling smoke and steam-clouds, the streak of ignited gases as something silver pulled itself away from gravity and into the skies, from the world that was my cradle to the space that was made for my aspirations. 'Laurie,' my mother would say, 'you should try some other games.' But that was what I liked the best.

There were gasps as the first image came: a razed city, empty and, but for wisps of smoke and the settling of dust, utterly still. Untimely Dead lay face-down in grey dust. Some of them were hideously burned. Familiar, yet still shocking: I felt sick, as usual. I caught myself thinking, not again, can't we forget, aren't we supposed to be on holiday? Sorry. I managed to look away. Most of the other passengers sat hunched, their eyes sliding desperately across the screen as if searching for a safe place; a few had closed their eyes. The man in front of me turned carefully round and winked; I felt myself blush, turned back to the screen.

A rapid sequence of war-stills followed; explosions, weaponry, weeping mothers, men in trenches – and the sound track became discordant, staccato sounds suggesting shots, screams, sirens. The last still, a tank, came suddenly to life and seemed to lumber towards us.

Again, gasps. There didn't seem to be anyone in it. There were no windows; the guns pointed straight at us, bigger and bigger. My whole body was tensed against the impact. I knew that if I said something aloud, even gibberish, the spell would be broken, but somehow I didn't dare. At the last moment, it vanished.

I began to feel quite angry. We know all this, I wanted to say. It's a day of celebration and we're supposed to be on holiday. I turned to try to see Stella, who'd wanted to look out of the window.

'Are you all right?' whispered the steward. I nodded, and turned back. *You have to see. You have to know*, they used to say at school, and probably still do.

We were shown a large room full of soberly dressed men, seated at great distance from each other around an enormous polished table. People kept coming in and out. Photographs were being taken. The image was recut and repeated with different men, at different tables. There was a babble of voices competing with the music. The odd words stood out: invisible enemies, imbalance, capability, assurance, verification; the sequence of words repeated itself many times, meaningless, enervating; it seemed to be getting faster and higher.

'When is it supposed to be?' I asked Kim petulantly. My sense of pre-war history was vague. I remembered it as a sequence of ghastly images and phrases in a childish voice – The time of Fifty Wars – The time of Unacceptable Risk – and so on. Kim hesitated. Now some of the men, with women beside them and some kind of Surveillance in attendance, were walking through wide streets lined with eager-seeming people standing behind striped barriers. They reached over the barrier to shake hands with children, they kissed babies and accepted flowers.

'It's the Arms Race, you know –' said someone behind us, and another voice, irritated, contradicted, 'No, it's after that. It's the Time of Talk without Treaty. You know, stalling. End of century.'

'Ssh.'

We were in a city square at dusk. It must have been winter, for all the trees were bare, and huge quantities of paper and cartons blew about on a wind we in the plane couldn't hear for music: everywhere litter, wrapping itself around trees, racing along the ground, winding itself into tight knots only to rise like hundreds of runaway kites. Down one of the broad avenues that led to the square came a silent procession of tiny lights. People were carrying candles in glass jars, hunched over to protect them from the wind. They began to fill the square. They just stood with their candles. Suddenly there was a magnificent blaze of light, then another, another, and blazing streaks of fire as flying papers ignited. The camera moved in close. With an air of great tranquillity, a young woman doused herself in fuel, then struck a match. She threw her arms up, her face contorted, and then was lost in light. I gasped and leaned forwards, trying to see her through it. I wanted to bring her back.

The square was ablaze with hundreds of human candles, twisting and jerking, some even running a little before collapsing into bonfires on the ground. The edges of the square were sketched with traceries of burning twigs. Other people were throwing themselves beneath army trucks and tanks that rolled in from the other avenues, and the procession still poured in, but faster, flickering, as if pushed from behind. In the midst of it all were children, holding banners and placards high above their heads: 'The risk is too great' – 'We won't wait' – 'Give me a future' – even as flames licked at the edges, ate up the words and swept them into the sky, they stood impassive, even smiling.

'They died for us,' someone said huskily. 'They died Untimely.'

Even I could tell that this was the Burning Protest, when enormous petitions were signed – millions of names in millions of different hands, the sketchy, the illegible, the underlined; when there were flocks of defectors, east to west, west to east, south to north, north to south – even the most patriotic began to hate their own governments for their deafness and inertia, for the pain of a risk grown unbearable. Studies were made which eventually defined statistically how much risk any population would tolerate, but on screen it was obvious: no one could bear to stay where they were, many could hardly bear to live.

I was crying.

'It's only history,' said Kim. I felt as if I had been there. They were so brave. They looked tired, thinly dressed, small; they were swallowed up in silent fire and the screen dissolved in a blaze of light. The music, which had been thin and sad, began to gather itself confidently together, signalling that we were nearly there, had nearly crossed that line that separated now from Time Before. We were racing inexorably towards the Accidental Launch, the Unfought War, when minute after minute, one by one, mounting up to almost half an hour, most of the people in the world thought they were going to die, fast or slow, in agony or oblivion.

At least, I sometimes think, they were together then, when they thought they were paying their Price. At least they had decided. At least they knew it wasn't a fair one and remembered they hadn't been asked. At least they hadn't been *saved*. At least they knew.

On screen: daylight, a street full of upturned faces wiped void with terror. A sky, clear, cloudless, empty . . . the sound of sirens.

'It didn't happen, Laurie,' Kim reminded me. But even behind closed eyelids I could see it and I knew what it was like. One moment you'd want to hide, the next to embrace the nearest person and stroke their hair, weeping, then to die before it happened; there would be a sudden terrible silence and then the wail of sirens and I too would be gaping at the sky, nothing to do but wait, stricken. The chaos of music became one huge chord, then snapped itself suddenly off. Children had been screaming and were now struggling for breath.

Kim nudged me.

'The bad stuff's over,' he whispered. All about us people were shifting in their seats, stretching a little, offering relieved, watery smiles to the stewards as they distributed tissues and sweet biscuits made in the shape of a dove. As our pulses slowed, the chord separated itself into tight strands and played on, stirring, sublime, and the screen stayed blank for a minute on end, as if, like us, it was recovering.

A dove flew into focus, then wheeled across the screen. A title appeared in white, as if painted by its wing-tip: *The Coming of Peace*. It signalled that we would be rescued now, and there would be words, and everything would be in perfect colour; no more nightmare monochrome; no need now to steel ourselves, shut our eyes, nor to look so hard. We unwrapped our biscuits as four faces we all knew as well as our own slowly materialized: Briggs, Karancheck, Minito, Ellulah. Now there was a faint murmur of conversation from the audience, and one or two people went to the toilet.

> At the last minute of the last hour, these four men, the Peace-makers, averted the disaster by diverting the missiles to far orbits, whence they will never return.

'When I was a child,' I said to Kim, 'that always used to worry me. If I heard a loud noise, I used to think they had fallen back.'

'Me too –' the steward said as he collected our biscuit wrappers, wiped away the crumbs, and we laughed.

> They sat down for two days and two nights and achieved what thousands of meetings had failed to achieve in the past, indeed more than had ever been attempted, the *International Force's Treaty*.

Fanfare. We saw them, their faces pouched, their skin speckled, eyes hooded, their old-man bodies laced with the scars of life-prolonging surgery; they were so old they hardly looked human (I suppose *they* just missed paying the Price). And they kissed each other and waved on a balcony, and flocks of white and silver balloons were released, and the crowds broke and joined, threw their arms up, roared and wept: the sound filled the plane, as it must have done that air, rose like an immense and ever accumulating cloud pouring into the sky. There were cameras everywhere, fireworks and streamers; people tore their clothes off, threw things in the air; those were days of dancing, weeping – the camera showed us faces that seemed as if they would split for joy, and I, my previous resentment dissolved in a warm welter of gratitude and guilt, fought back my own tears.

> This will be the most recorded event in human history. We, the representatives of world powers formerly in continual and escalating conflict, are proud to be the authors of such an agreement as this. It is a far-reaching treaty founded on our common desires as nations; its aim is to eliminate conflict at all levels and to ensure that hostilities are never again commenced, nor even contemplated.

It was the end and the beginning.

Trolleys were being wheeled down the aisles. There were sandwiches and white-iced cake.

'They don't look like us, do they?' someone remarked, 'they're sort of like enormous children.'

'He's ugly, that man, ugly and old.' Stella's voice was subdued, but penetrating.

> We have learned a bitter lesson hard; yet it is our view that history has brought us to this point, and that without what has gone before, without the knowledge of our potential for destruction, we would not be in a position to realize our potential for progress. We are closing one book with a sigh of relief and opening another, the pages of which are yet to be written.

Oh, I remember it. Word for word, what was said. My heart aches. It's harder to remember what happened.

They *were* different, those people in the crowds, they seemed more distinguished each from the other. Particularly women: their skin and hair colours were strongly marked, their faces and bodies all seemed to tell different stories. They aged unevenly and, of course, many were very, very old indeed. As I watched their celebrations, I tried to follow individuals in the crowd. I wanted to see what they did, where they were going. . . . One by one, I lost them. Of course, lives were more differentiated then. Some were so poor and short they were scarcely lives at all. Some women bore huge families; children died. Some people worked all the time, some not at all. There were hundreds of languages, a babble of difference, and the Treaty, the glorious Treaty, was translated into all of them.

> We have pressed our ears to the heartbeat of the times. We have broken our chains. As brothers in peace, we will move together into the space beyond our world, which belongs to no one and to all. There will be neither violence nor fear. We know ourselves, seek to conquer only what is beyond. . . .

Briggs' voice faltered. He was crying. His words echoed, and were drowned in whistles and cheers. The music skipped and careened as the crowd gathered into huge circles, widening and rushing inwards, clinging together as tears washed away the last shadows and stains left by decades of bewilderment and rage, as they ran splashing into the sea, gathered together to eat, drink wine on the grass; they rolled in snow, clambered into vehicles and cruised through sunlit streets. Young and old together, they let themselves be thrown in the air and caught in nets of arms. They weren't thinking about the Price. Perhaps then they didn't even know of it.

Suddenly it was quiet, and we saw a young woman sitting alone in a summer garden with a dovecote. She pushed the hair back from her face and smiled right at us; it was as if she was right there in the aeroplane. The birds cooed contentedly, a warm, bubbling sound.

> 'It was the most beautiful thing I've ever heard,' she said, softly, her eyes crinkling up. 'I cried. A dream come true.'

We clapped. Over an hour had passed, everyone looked exhausted. The screen was dead. One by one the blinds were raised, and we all sought the windows gratefully. The plane was beginning to decelerate. The vibration in the main cabin felt stronger and coarser. We were slipping below the last wisps and swathes of cloud. An island came into view below, a softly indented triangle of green set in an enormous expanse of spangled blue. Around it a line of white, another of indigo. Small clouds gathered on the windward side of the island and cast shadows on the sea. The plane wheeled in around the coastline, showing beaches, cliffs and bays. Below us was one of the last patches of the natural earth, displayed to our view, simplified by distance, its colours and contours burnished by the sun. It was utterly beautiful, and yet I felt strangely apprehensive; my hand lay as a fist in Kim's. He stroked my fingers open.

Closer still, and the tree-tops were thrown into soft

relief; the crests of waves, the mobile patterns of eddies and currents, came suddenly into sharp and brilliant focus. Small tracks and two rivers separated the vegetation like partings in a head of hair.

One or two people had tears in their eyes. The middle-aged woman in front of me turned to the young man at her side and said, 'I'll never have the words to say how I feel, or how much.'

'You've said that before,' he replied.

The stewards gathered together in a line and stood respectfully still and silent: the Anniversary Speech was to be broadcast as we circled the island and then descended. A child began to wail. The voice that emerged from the speakers was a man's, soft yet precise, almost tender.

> We celebrate today the immense achievements of our recent history. At the last minute of the last hour, all opposing powers became as one . . .

The plane tilted and for a few seconds I could see nothing but sky. I wish we would never arrive, I thought with sudden clarity, I wish we'd plunge into the sea. I'm scared.

> . . . Treaty will be remembered until the end of time . . . the weapons which almost ended the human race are now gathered together and guarded by the International Force until such time as they can be neutralized . . .

Everyone knew the words of the speech by heart, and some followed them soundlessly with their lips.

> Our children grow up proud, determined and optimistic, we sleep without nightmares, we have saved ourselves from ourselves by a supreme act of will and understanding . . .

My ears hurt and it all seemed strangely far away.

> Look down at the earth below and do not forget . . . all powers became as one . . .

The Anthem played. We were served with Anniversary champagne, bottle after bottle of tingling dry wine, expertly opened and poured, singing on the tongue. People began to laugh and chatter, exchanging names, imagining the coming days of idleness.

'It means so much –' the woman in front was saying.

'Don't start crying, we've arrived,' said the young man.

The land below hurtled into life-size. Wheels slammed into the runway, our seats pressed into our backs.

The tiny airport was fringed with tall trees. It was very quiet. As we emerged from the plane the sky began to deepen, and the very faintest shadow of a moon appeared low in the sky. The air was warm and smelled of flowers. Our bags would be carried to the tents already erected for us. I'd seen pictures of these: pastel-coloured domes and pyramids, each with its own flag for easy recognition, arranged in rows either side of grassy walkways; fully equipped with luxury bedding, lights, music centres and so on. Nothing but the thinnest cloth between you and the sky, they'd said to me when I booked, a once in a lifetime experience.

The bar and restaurant in the harbour were open, we were told, and tonight everything would be free. 'Welcome,' the staff kept saying. 'Welcome to Island Paradise.' Kim and I climbed the tree-lined path arm in arm, silent; we could hear tiny waves breaking on the beach.

We were shown to our pale-green tent just as night fell. It felt strange, bending down to enter, pulling the fasteners apart, and feeling the walls move when we brushed against them. We switched on the lamp and changed our clothes. We could hear other people doing the same, fumbling with the fasteners and unfamiliar controls, dropping things, laughing. At night, I thought, we'll be able to hear everyone breathe. I imagined it, a huge collective sigh and pause, regular, magnificent.

'You look lovely,' whispered Kim.

My flesh must have been soft and resilient then, my face ignorantly smooth: fit, almost, for Martina's wall display. Now, beneath the coating of lotion, it is scarred and blotched, some parts have never healed, still weep. Then, I remember wearing a large straw hat, not on my head but dangling behind it, a kind of frame to my face. Now, it's a beret or a cap whenever I go out; I stuff my hair inside to conceal it. I was young, now I'm old.

I've cheated myself out of a few years as well, for although I'm only forty-eight my card says sixty, and that's what counts. I'm over Time and haven't got long. Time Before, people who lived to twice my age were the object of admiration, wonder and envy. They received letters of congratulation from world leaders, and touching tributes from their neighbours. Now it's different, we have our Timely Deaths. I'm expected to depart gently, unaided by chemicals, bullets or other mechanical means. Do It Yourself. The Timely Dead are not mourned; no looking back as, vaporized and already forgotten, they slip voluntarily into the air we breathe. Retirement from work is, after all, a period of adjustment. A time when we can sum ourselves up, say goodbye, *let go* – The Future's a Young Country, as the phrase goes, So Long as The Power Lasts. A Timely Death is not a sad death, Martina used to tell her clients. But mine isn't coming easy.

I wonder about the origins of our easy surrender to our own deaths. After all, we're not allowed to kill. You don't see it on the Anniversary films, how people took that bit of news. As if that part of the Treaty was drowned in the cheering, the relief. Did no one protest?

It's late to be asking this sort of question. I've wasted such an awful quantity of years, before we went, since we came back. Now I can't sleep. Every night I wake up at about this time. The swish of traffic and the uneven breath of distant winds remind me of the oceans we crossed, of the island, the archipelago and the journey back; yet I've said to myself for years that I do not want to put to sea again, nor to travel in the air. I've told myself, forget. I fetch a glass of water, I pull the curtain aside to look at the night as I drink. I still have the photographs; I developed them myself because he would not: I agitated the tray and slowly the scratched negatives yielded images, light and dark growing into shape. The island, his mother, the man. Me. H. Darker and clearer in the red half-light, the hum of the extractor fan. Part of me always hoped things would change, or somehow end, after our return. Sometimes I think they are beginning to, but the signs are very small: a flicker on the face on the screen, cries in the night. Like just now, I'd swear I heard a woman shout close by, 'It's not true. You always lie!'

I recognized her voice, I've passed the time of day rather unsatisfactorily with her on several occasions. Petite, with slightly bulging grey eyes. She works in transportation planning, and always holidays at the Lakes. And I heard someone answer her in a quiet, reassuring mumble; I recognized the tone of his voice as well. If I should hear tomorrow, next week, that she slipped a polythene bag over her lover's head while he slept – it's illegal, it's unspeakable, unheard of, yet, admit it – I wouldn't be surprised. I've not seen him, only heard the even words that flow from his lips in the lingering hours of the night when I pull the curtain aside to look at the street, surprised that everything still stands, sometimes thinking I've caught a glimpse of figures running, a whirr of wheels, even the quiet phut! of a silenced shot. I hear his voice; it comes to the ear milk-soft, yet curdles inside, hangs suspended. It is the same voice which gives us the thrice daily announcements, and tells us it is safe to cross the trafficway, when to fasten our seatbelt. It is, I imagine, the same voice that tells us in Age Counselling how to *let go*, and it's a good voice really, so calm, so considerate in its modulation – but it won't answer to the charge of lying, and it drives you mad.

I don't think I'm the only one that stands looking out at night. I hear other windows eased open so as not to disturb. I think I see other shadows behind the blinds.

But maybe I imagine even that, perverse, to comfort myself. After all, what is there to stop things going on for ever, so long as the Power lasts? And it does; we're beginning extraction on Planet Three: stations, converters and factories are nearing completion, soon Power from Three will be flowing along lengths and coils of gossamer cable, and we'll breathe easy for another hundred years. The young compete for the status of employment off earth, or Planet One, as it's becoming known. Planet One: makes you think of all the other infinite numbers that might follow. New beginnings, further away; generally, people are not interested in ends, but I am: mine for a start. It won't be long before I receive my first invitation to see an Age Counsellor, and I don't know what I'll do or say.

H stirs in his sleep, but I know he won't wake. Once I nearly killed him. Illegal. Unspeakable. Unheard of. Then again, he was once prepared to let me die, and he'd be dead twice over but for me. Now, we have become each other's world in the absence of a better one. I look at him and wonder why we have stayed together. We share secrets, but then there's never been any question of betrayal. And for some years we've cherished a fantasy, which we call our plan.

In it, H is sleeping, or I am, it can go either way – H is sleeping, lightly. He's very old; his hair is grey, his skin carved with lines. Our mutual attraction has long ceased to puzzle me. I'm older still, perhaps a hundred. I watch him, thinking of the secret past, treasuring it: my fingers in and on him, my hands about his throat, his turned back – a see-saw struggle that's brought its own kind of peace. I am glad that we could have blown the world apart and that we didn't; the sounds of the sea are in my ears.

I touch his shoulder. He wakes, rolls on his back and looks at me.

'Now,' I say. He continues looking, his face lost in shadows. I touch it; it's rough like mortar, but warm.

'You're sure?' I nod, words desert me. The sounds of the sea are in my ears. He stands up.

'There's a little light by the window,' he says.

The end slips in through a pinprick in the skin, a full-stop on the page. We return to the bed. We lie in desire but touch only to know, remind, then forget. Our breathing is shallow. I am happy. I know each pulse-beat is a little less, though I cannot feel it yet.

This is our end, as simple and calm as two different shades of blue laid side by side: sea, sky. Many years ago I wanted the plane to crash into the sea; now, much later, I want this. I cradle his head, he supports my neck. We are growing heavy. We are very alone, together. We are escaping again. Eventually, Surveillance will cut the lock and find us, but we will be gone. Quite soon there will be a last breath, this one perhaps.

'I'm afraid,' we say together.

'You're not,' we answer, and we are not.

We worked this out together, a long time ago. But it's no good for me any more. I change the subject when he mentions it, or I hold him in my arms dishonestly, as if in sympathy, or I smile and say, 'Not yet.' I'm tight and tense and don't want to die, not any way, not even our way. I'm waiting for something else. I watch the announcements every day. I try to commit their contents to memory. I wonder how long I've got. I want to dream of elsewhere, but come back in the end to death. How, when? Why, *for whom*?

⋆

'Laurie,' H says, 'sit still. Have a drink. Calm down. Give up. It's too big.'

'Are you telling me to *let go* as well?' That throws him for a bit.

'No,' he says. 'I'm not telling you anything –' He's said that before, I think, to someone else. I was there. I heard it. 'Forget it. Let's have some peace. Put some music on. Have you eaten?' Often I answer no, because then he will make me something, and will be awake longer.

'Peace?' I say. 'That's fine from you! I can't forget. I can't sleep – why me?'

'I sleep. Leave me out of it, please. And I wish you'd put your stuff away in the drawers instead of spreading it about like – like that –' His voice is always infuriatingly even, the sense is all in the actual words, nothing in the tone. 'And stop scribbling on the walls. There's a machine for writing, for Christ's sake; we have to pay for it, you might as well use it.'

We don't use much of what we pay for in the rent, which is low, because of me. Not long though, before it starts to go up, telling me I've had my Time, charging me because I haven't paid. We keep more or less to the same room, the one with the view of the street. The units are empty; I like to keep things neat, but out, visible. The screen, of course, we use for personal shopping, but rarely entertainment. There's the bed, huge: we're both small, it swamps us. Various other appliances which came with the place I have disconnected and placed in a row along the far wall, their leads and connectors wound and taped down: massager, mini-lightshow, fitness centre. There's my table, facing the window, the writing machine, which anyway I do use most of the time; just now and then I feel like touching what I do, having my hand make the shapes.

'It looks crazy,' he says.

'So what? No one sees. It comes off. If you bring someone home I'll gladly change it. Only needs a coat of paint.'

'I'm not bringing anyone home,' he says, ever so slightly sharp, 'don't start that, please. You know it's impossible. We couldn't carry it off.' He gestures vaguely at himself, then me. 'There's only us. Don't you go on about what happened. You know what we can do –' he means our plan – 'I'm waiting, you know what for. I don't want to hear anything about the past. Don't interfere with me, please.' The bottle's empty, he puts it carefully down the chute. I imagine it, going down, the impact. I feel sick.

'You'd've been glad if *she'd* interfered a bit, wouldn't you?' I say. 'Can't accuse you of consistency.' He looks through me, as if he hasn't heard. 'You didn't used to be like this,' I complain. No, he was something else, perhaps worse. He leans back, shuts his eyes as if to sleep, just like that. He can. 'No!' I say loudly, urgent, 'I didn't eat today.' My heart pounds. Frustration, mixed with a kind of hope, almost excitement: one day he will not sleep, one day – what is it I want? Tears? Tomorrow morning, he will rise on time, clean up his face and look as if nothing has happened.

He goes to work before I'm awake. He is meticulously tidy, leaving the bathroom just so. Before he goes, he prepares me a meal on a tray, and places it in the bathroom, balanced across the hand-basin. I make the most of my morning bath, hot, cold, steam or spa, according to how I feel. There are no windows in the bathroom, and I don't bother with the light. I shut the door, turn on the water, and eat my meal by touch in the dark as the room fills with steam. Then I climb in and blank out for half an hour; it's a pleasure more reliable than sleep. Night. Morning. Night, water. I dry myself, judge the weather, dress, cream my face and go to watch the announcements.

Good morning. Today, it was announced . . . Three times a day, every adult living or working here in Central City, and countless places like it, comes together in front of a public telescreen. Schools have their own. My nearest is in the square just at the end of the street. It is one of the newest and best, three metres or so across, and angled slightly downwards so that when we crane our necks to look, the eyes of the people on the screen meet perfectly with ours. If I didn't go, I'd be able more or less to hear it from our room. But it's not often I don't go. There's a kind of compulsion. It needn't happen. We could view at home, if they changed the channels. We could record, and watch days' or weeks' worth at a time – but we don't. Everyone goes. If you're working, it's time off, of course. If you're working at home, it's when you see other people. You can meet your friends, you get to recognize strangers, sometimes exchange a few words. The music stops and the announcements are preceded by silence and blank screens. *Good afternoon. Today, it was announced* . . . Vehicles stop in the street. Machines are switched off, lovers pull apart, and even I drag myself to the lift. If you listen carefully, you can hear a high-pitched hum emanating from the screen, an excited sound. Everyone wants to know: new achievement, a snippet of progress. To see: pictures of ourselves. But mostly it's nothing much – minor discoveries, new products available, breaches of industrial or personal safety law, reorganization of the manufacturing base and so on. Heard, forgotten. I don't go to meet people. I go in the vain hope that something's happened, is happening. Often I walk home dull, disappointed, and wonder why I went. *Good evening. Tonight, it was announced* . . . As if nothing ever happened. But it did.

'I didn't eat today,' I repeat. Another pause.

'I don't believe you,' H says, without opening his eyes. Some days this would make me cry; but not today. I write it down. Full-stop. End of conversation. Still, as such it is better than the other exchanges I can have, in the Residential lift, or when we wait in the square for the announcements. For instance, today, with a woman I've seen many times from the window, coming home late, arm in arm with her partner.

'Hello,' I'll say. 'Ground? How's work?' The doors meet. She's my prisoner until we reach ground.

'Good. But I'm trying to get into space, along with half the world.'

'Oh. Why?'

'Excitement I suppose. It's the fastest growing area.'

'But what's it for?' I always ruin it. She looks bewildered.

'It's a new beginning,' she says, checking the indicator, wanting to escape from me.

'And what else are you doing?'

'Not much, we're saving for our main holiday.'

'Where –'

'Not sure. Snowy Peaks. Golden Desert. Island Paradise, wherever.'

I feel she doesn't want to talk. I grow self-conscious. I know soon there will be a faint shudder, the doors will open, and my companion will hasten away. I know my clothes aren't quite right. It's not for lack of credit – I make an effort to choose something new each month, I dedicate half a day to it, studying each item several times before keying in my choice – but I feel I don't blend in.

'Happy?' I ask, trying to keep my voice sweet.

'Why yes, of course. Very.'

'What d'you think of –?' But we're down; she has to go. No one asks me anything. No one volunteers any information or comment. I see them running their eyes quickly over my face. *I wonder how old* – that's what they're thinking. *Pay the Price, damn you.* I'm stuck with H.

Each night, when at last I know I'll sleep, I check the apartment over. The Power supply, the water, the locks. I make sure that anything I've been using is back in position, next to other like objects, in a row; that both sheets are neatly tucked in all round, the quilt is evenly spread. . . . I dip my finger in the remains of my glass of water, touch the back of H's neck with it, then suck it dry. The same every night. I mark him. He's in my keeping. It'll be all right till tomorrow. Finally, briefly, I'm at peace as I ease myself in. I never dream.

The Lens

The coffee was good. Kim and I sat in the beach café under striped umbrellas. It was very hot and bright, almost overpowering. We smiled vaguely at other holiday-makers as they squeezed past us with their trays. Most of us were a little tired after the previous day's journey, and the first night under canvas. 'Sleep well?' people enquired of each other, smiling knowingly. The walls of our tent had shrunk and billowed with a breeze we couldn't feel. I'd lain watching them, and then I must have slept, because that was all I could remember.

'What would you like to do?' Kim said, business-like. 'No amusement parks here. No laserplay. A few games in the bar though, and stuff to do at night. Apparently you can walk all the way round in a day. There are cliffs on one side of the harbour. There are nearly a thousand kinds of tree here. And a thriving insect community if I'm not mistaken. No buildings except the airport and the bar complex. Water-sports of course if you'd like –'

I lowered my sunglasses. 'I think I'd like to sleep for ever,' I said. We were both startled.

'What d'you mean?'

'I'm tired,' I said, 'that's all. I don't want to do anything.'

'But we're on holiday!' he said, squinting at me because the sun was in his eyes. 'Are you sick of me? Why don't you spend a night with someone else, provided it's safe . . .? Best to, if that's what you feel like.'

'I know that. It's not –' I said harshly, and then felt very tender towards him, weak with it, as if warm liquid was draining painlessly from me.

'Sorry. Let's just walk a little way,' I said, 'and lie down somewhere nice.'

We lay hand in hand in the sun for several hours. There was no one else around. I felt terrible, and wondered about going to the medical office. At one point I began to cry with my eyes closed. He didn't notice, we were covered in sweat. Afterwards, I felt better.

Towards late afternoon, when the light became yellowish and we started to have shadows, two men, perhaps father and son, came running on the beach. At first they seemed to be running together, then it looked as if the younger was racing, or chasing, the older.

'Bit hot for that,' said Kim lazily.

They ran into the sea. Initially the older man shot ahead, swimming smoothly, while the young man seemed to flounder and splash. Though there wasn't a breath of wind, the red flag was flying.

'Probably forgot to take it down,' said Kim, following my gaze. Whenever I was silent, he used to break into my thoughts like that, guess what they were, stifle them with some comment or other.

Though they were very distant, it seemed as if the young one had caught up. I couldn't see properly. There was a lot of splashing and some shouts.

'Kim –'

'Just mucking about.'

'One of them may be in trouble.'

'Well, the other one's there to help.'

He pushed me back on the rug. After a few minutes, I sat up again, wiping his saliva from my face. One swimmer had nearly reached the shore. The second followed very slowly, and waded as soon as he could stand. It was the older man. He stood in the shallows for a while, hands on knees, breathing hard, and then began to walk back the way they had come.

'See?' said Kim.

'It looked like . . . some kind of attack,' I said. 'He was holding his head under.' My heart was beating faster.

'Don't be silly. You say the strangest things!' said Kim, trying again to push me back. This time, I felt more like I wanted to.

'We never do this at home,' I said.

'No, that's only natural. We're not so young. I just don't feel like it very often –'

'Nor do I,' I said. 'It's only for kids really, isn't it, and psychos, holiday-makers perhaps?'

'Right. We can go home now,' I joked afterwards. I'd bitten him on the shoulder till he bled, and not apologized. When we got back to the site, he covered the marks with his shirt, as if ashamed.

Everyone agreed that Island Paradise was as beautiful as the brochure said. We woke in the pale glow of the tents, already breathing fresh air, smelling the sea. As the sun strengthened, overhanging leaves made patterns of shadow on the tent and our skin. We walked on narrow paths through towering trees. We stood on the cliffs and gazed out to sea.

'You're quiet.'

Daily we went to the beach.

I let sand pour slowly between my fingers; it was coarse, made from tiny fragments of multicoloured shell. I could hear the damp friction of skin on skin as Kim readjusted his dozing position, the dry rustle of the sand he displaced, the quiet murmur of music escaping from nearby headphones. I could feel footsteps in the sand and the thud of breakers on the shore; everything I saw or heard seemed to fix me, I was there, anchored, pinned, I wanted not to be. I realized this sharp and painful desire to escape had been with me ever since we stepped out of the plane. At the same time it seemed that there was nowhere to go: the island was a small, waterlocked piece of land; our return tickets were booked for twenty days ahead. I tried to let my mind out to the thin line between sea and air, nothing but blue, tried to make figures out of clouds – but something would always bring me back: Kim would laugh in his sleep, a slow staccato chuckling, half lost in his throat – and just as there's always something to do, so even the sky would seem nowhere to go. The sky was part of the earth, dotted with satellites, stations, debris, signals; zoned and demarcated, used, mapped and plotted: how to dream of elsewhere? Someone'd been there. Here: the island, so small and fixed, a floating cage. I felt as if I was fighting with my own skin. I need help, I thought, I'm ill. But I didn't go to seek it; I lay still and heavy on the shelldust beach.

Behind us a young couple made love on a large rug cast over the sand. The man was on top, his face screwed tight, eyes shut. The woman was wearing headphones. Her fingers bit hard into his back. I wondered what they were thinking about. I thought about the two men in the sea, drowning.

Children kicked footballs and splashed in the shallows. My mat was soaked with sweat, I felt it pressing basket patterns into my skin. I wanted the bitter biting sea like I sometimes wanted sleep, sudden and strong as an intravenous injection; but the red flag was still flying, *unsafe to bathe*, hard to breathe.

I counted the days as they passed, and the nights. I thought alternately: this was a mistake, or there's something wrong with me. Then, as now, I didn't want anyone to know.

There was a free drink if you wore fancy dress in the bar. Many of the children went as space travellers or Surveillance, though one small girl went in a skirt with a band of feathers round her head and patterns painted on her face. I asked her what she was supposed to be. 'I don't know,' she said. 'I saw it somewhere once.'

Along with most of the adults, Kim and I had no idea what to wear, so we went in our ordinary clothes and had to pay for our drinks. We watched the children.

Kim took my hand. 'I only want to be who I am,' he whispered.

There was a squeal, followed by wailing. The little girl with feathers in her hair had stabbed a space traveller in the rump with a sharpened stick. A small spot of blood was spreading on his brilliant white and too big trousers. The music was switched off, and everyone turned to stare.

'Why did you do that, Stella?' her mother said in a voice smooth as silk. So that's her, I thought.

'I don't know,' she said; her face colouring, she stared fixedly at her feet.

'Did you want to hurt him?'

Stella's whispered 'No' was barely audible.

'Did you want to upset all these people?'

Stella tried to turn away from us but her father stood behind her, his hands on her shoulders. She buried her head in his stomach; he prised it away, and turned her back round.

'No,' she said. There was a long silence. She grew limp. Her eyes filled with tears. Her father let go of her and pushed her gently forwards.

'I'm sorry,' she said to the space traveller. His face was sullen. He clutched his wound. I felt peculiar, realized I wanted to laugh.

'Thank you. That's fine,' he muttered. Still the group waited.

'Come on!' said Stella's mother, urgently. Stella turned to face the gathered crowd, her face-paint streaked, her jaw clenched.

'I am sorry,' she said, looking somewhere above our heads, and the music began again. Stella's father took the stick and broke it into small pieces. Her mother, silent, led her out of the bar, plucking at the rest of the costume.

'If we had one it wouldn't be like that, I'm sure,' said Kim as we danced, bathed in purple light. I pretended not to hear. I liked Stella, and wished I could have cheered her up.

Later that night I was woken after several hours by the

sounds of an argument, and footsteps in the dry grass. In the total darkness of the tent the voices seemed like a visitation or a transmission; it was an effort to imagine them coming from real people. I lay without moving; I didn't wake Kim.

'He's only come to see if I'm all right. It's just something he does,' a woman said, her voice wheedling.

'Interfering,' a man replied. I knew who they were when he spoke: the young man and older woman who had sat in front of us in the plane.

'He just loves me. It's only natural.'

'That's a joke,' he said, 'he hates your guts.'

'Don't. Please. You didn't used to be like this.' Her voice was a thin stream of misery.

'Stop crying!' he barked. 'Don't touch me!'

'What's all of this about?' the woman said next. 'I don't care, just tell me.'

Someone was running in the grass; there were sounds of sobbing, grunts, tearing cloth.

'Please,' the woman said.

They were fighting! I threw the flap open. What should I do? Raise the alarm? Call for Surveillance? But surely I'd made a mistake. I could see nothing, but the air outside was soft and cool. I did nothing. I wanted to hear what would happen next.

'Why should I? I need my glasses.' The man was breathing heavily. He seemed to be very close. 'They were in this bloody tent, they've probably been broken.'

'I can't find them! I'm sorry.' The woman's voice rose to a wail. Then there was silence. I was about to get out of the tent when she spoke again.

'I just want to *know*,' she said, suddenly calm, and her words were like cold water in my face. I was certain for the first time that I was awake.

He did not answer. Kim's breathing filled the tent. In, out: the tent was an enormous lung in someone else's body. I slept again, unmoving, blank.

*

Such sleep. Thick sleep, the sleep of the innocent, the dead, and H. In. Out. Regular. No caught breath, stifled snores, grinding teeth, muttering – I shouldn't envy, but I do. How come I'm the one to sit awake, watching? I imagine H's sleep as a lake of warm black oil. He floats on it. I'm the guard. He trusts me for his safety. He says he wants to die with me, holding hands, not scared. On the bottom of the lake is something that would change all this. To find it, though, I'd have to abandon my post, and I'm too afraid.

We were sitting at our usual table in the beach café. 'Ready now?' asked Kim. I shook my head as if lost in thought over my impulse-bought postcards. They seemed such a sweet idea, but I couldn't think what to say. The argument in the tent replayed itself in my head. The white rectangles, curling slightly in the heat, dazzled my eyes. *'I just want to know –'* Kim turned back to the telescreen.

'They're going to intensify the clean-up research programme,' he reported. 'The Treaty's been signed over a century and they've got nowhere. In Pesticides we have to come up with two or three products a month. These joint efforts are seldom efficient. Perhaps it isn't possible to get rid of the damn stuff when it comes down to it. Why don't we just brick it up and forget about it?' He paused, looked up at the sky, squinting. 'But it's better than nothing. They're trying. It's better than before. They must know what they're doing. It's all progress.' He checked that I had still written nothing on the cards, took one, holding it by the corner. 'Waste of money and resources,' he said, 'after all, it's quicker to call people. Gimmick.' He smiled cheerfully, then looked back up at the screen.

A queue was forming at the service counter. I noticed a young man wearing, unbelievably in such heat, a thick oiled wool sweater. His hair was cut close. He was short and very thin, angular; his shoulder blades rose and fell exaggeratedly as he picked up his cup and spoon. A camera and assortment of lenses and meters were slung across his back. He seemed to be alone. He chose an unoccupied table in a far corner of the courtyard and immediately took out the camera. He made a series of careful adjustments, finally rocking his body fractionally back and forth. I watched him with all the intensity that he devoted to focussing the camera. I followed the line of the lens to see what interested him so much. There was nothing, only holiday-makers, dirty cups, birds picking at crumbs. Finally, after holding himself still for a few moments, he placed the camera on the table without pressing the shutter. He didn't notice me.

'Stuck?' asked Kim, gesturing at the postcards. He came round to stand behind me, covered my eyes with his hands and kissed my neck. I pushed his hands away, but by then the man was gone. We went to the beach. There was no sign of him there. Kim wrote the postcards, I don't know if they were ever sent.

'I'm glad we've come before we were too old
for the journey.'
'I wish we could stay for a year.'
'Feels as if time's stood still.'
'Once in a lifetime.'
'Always glad, of course, to go home.'
'We'll have the photographs.'
'I'll tell them all it's not to be missed.'
'Paradise indeed.'
'Never been happier in my life.'

Thud of the waves, *unsafe to bathe.*

I imagined drowning without struggle into a sleep from which I might never wake, or from which I would wake to find everything had gone. . . . I shut my eyes to welcome it, but it was impossible to go. I remembered the bartender. The scraps of conversation I overheard seemed sad or sinister; it was as if something hung about the edges of my sight. I wondered if I was dying Untimely. I thought of the man with the camera, his tiny gestures as he checked and tested, his concentration – I understood these things, I thought, but not why it was that I wanted to put myself before him as the object of that meticulous attention.

Later that morning, I saw him again, only a tiny distant figure, but I was absolutely sure it was him, crouched at the far end of the beach where the shore became narrow and vanished around a corner. I got to my feet and began running. I turned to wave to Kim, who sat upright and surprised, shading his eyes against the sun. The hot sand was soft and smothered my speed, but I sent it scattering behind me, running with my breasts held tight under the blue cloth. I was streamlined, polished, fast; I ran without pain or breathlessness, I could have run around the island if necessary. Now I could make him out properly. I could see the camera, pointing at me. I imagined myself running in brightness, framed by dark. Nearer, nearer, my two eyes looking into the glass one, my moving self brought by a series of specks to an essence inside the box, and from there his eyes would draw them out, would invert their upside-down image and reassemble the series of framed images back into rapid movement: Laurie, running, free, different, seen. I wanted the camera to see the bones and organs hiding under the jumper of flesh I would burn away by running. I wanted the man who held it to read me, test me, and to know what was wrong and what to do. I ran into the lens, I filled the field of view. My legs jammed to a standstill in the sand, shaking. I stood beside him, I wanted to look into his face.

He didn't turn to look at me. Unmoving, he held the camera, propped steady on one knee, his finger ready on the shutter. I was not included in his picture, perhaps I was even spoiling it. He was waiting for something else. I was breathing too hard, and too loud. Ashamed of my physical exhilaration beside his stillness, I stood there foolishly, unable to walk away.

I stared down at his short black hair, so thick that no scalp showed, and at his small hands, poised tense on the black and silver camera. He still wore the sweater. He was absolutely motionless. The sun was overhead, and neither of us cast a shadow.

'I'm busy. Perhaps we could meet later,' he said suddenly. He had an accent that might or might not have been, a strangeness that hid and flirted with his words. His voice wasn't unfriendly, but still he didn't look at me.

'Tomorrow morning,' he added. 'I'll be at the café.' Had he seen me watch him? I wanted him. I wasn't going to tell Kim.

This image of H as he seemed then, contained and powerful, and of myself, confused, waiting, wanting, frightened – it's so fixed in my mind, so ludicrously static. It's so untrue – yet I cherish it, and sometimes when I try to sleep before I am ready, it appears behind my closed eyes, bright and hot. That's how it was. I ran down the beach to see his face, and he wouldn't even look at me. I can stare at him all I like now. His breathing's light, sometimes it seems to stop for minutes on end. He sleeps that thick black sleep, lying on his back or curled like a child, a small shape beneath the covers. I love him and I hate him too, fiercely. And though *he* doesn't, I think every day about what he's done. I want to wake him up.

I walked slowly back down the exposed swathe of gleaming sand towards the clutter of colour at the sheltered end. To my right was a staggered line of craters in the beach, each with a tail of displaced sand, showing where I had run. Now, my marks were distinct footprints, much closer together. My legs were very tired. Looking up, I saw two people emerge from behind some rocks, walking towards the sea. There were several metres between them, but they kept the same pace. I recognized them: the couple who'd quarrelled in the night. A sense of dread came over me, a light but unrelenting pressure on my back. It was too late to avoid crossing their path. I stared at the young man, he of the glasses who'd slept with someone other than the woman old enough to be his mother. He was well proportioned and moved easily; his face might be described as beautiful, but was soured by arrogance. I felt hostile. A glance at the woman, her blonde waves just beginning to grey, her skin smarting under the sun, showed that she had only recently stopped crying.

'It's no use,' the man said to her as I passed in front of them, paying my stare back in kind.

When I turned to look again, the woman was walking parallel to the sea, towards the end of the beach where H still crouched motionless. The man was following in my direction and I quickened my pace.

'Hey!' he shouted after me, 'there's enough interfering around here, keep out of it.'

'What was all that about?' Kim asked. 'Was that someone up there? I didn't know you could run. . . . D'you think it's time for something to eat? Glad we came here? A pity life's not all like this, eh?' Smiling, he looked into my face, the deep brown of his eyes merged with the pupils into a sea of shiny darkness. For no reason that I could understand, I felt like striking him across the face.

I lay in the full afternoon sun, eyes closed, my cheek pressed to the sand; sounds burrowed straight into my inner ear, swelled, grew and scattered in my skull, noise and the odd cluster of words floating silly and harmless as balloons in languid air. Though I lay swimsuited and oiled as the rest, it was only a pretence of naked sameness, for my flesh hid bones, organs, thoughts, kept them secret, kept them mine. I felt them pressing into the shelldust beach and I knew I would find the camera man again, tomorrow morning in the beach café.

I went there very early. The umbrellas weren't yet up; there was still dew on the white painted tables and benches. He was already there, and I went to sit opposite him.

'I'm Laurie,' I said. I judged him to be about ten years younger than myself. The thump of my heart rocked my body, a kind of excitement, more than sex: a feeling like falling and freedom and fear.

'H,' he said, holding out his hand to shake, 'for Haley, which I don't like to use. H.' Again, something about his voice, like the intonation of a question, the scamper of something seen out of the corner of my eye, then gone.

'I left my friend Kim asleep,' I said. 'I couldn't sleep. I can't relax.'

'I've a yacht anchored offshore,' he said. 'I come in when the tide is right. I wouldn't stay here. Feels all wrong.'

'Why come at all then?'

He tapped the camera on the table. 'Photography. Decoration, commemorations, portraits. Anything. I've an unusual method, I get unusual results and there's a market for stills now. I've got a virtually unlimited travel permit. I wait – you've seen me – I don't waste film. There's a moment, a kind of peak, minute changes and movements build together, like pressure before a storm; there's a moment before it breaks apart, and that's when I try to press the shutter. I want a picture that speaks. And also, I love to be at sea, always have. Plus –' H stopped mid-sentence, his attention suddenly elsewhere. The woman from the tent was walking through the arch to my left. As she came out of the shadow, I noticed something peculiar about one side of her face, like a stain, and realized with a shock that it was in fact tinted face cream applied over a badly blacked eye and bruised cheek. She took a seat at our table, sponging the dew away with her handkerchief. H stared at her, as he finished speaking to me. 'Plus I'm here to see my mother. I've followed her, you might say, although –'

'All right, H,' the newcomer interrupted.

'Although I'm not in any sense with her as a companion. That's not my privilege. Laurie, my mother Jo.' She glanced at me briefly. They were utterly unlike.

'You were right, I grant you that,' Jo said to H. Her voice, tinged with resentment and the distress of physical pain, was harsh.

'Too damn right.' Her eye was more than half closed. Neither of them took any notice of me, yet I felt far from superfluous as I sat watching them, noticing how H's eyes had fastened themselves on Jo, pulling the space between them so tight that it seemed on the brink of collapse; how Jo on the other hand looked about her as she spoke, her good eye gazing into some vague, shifting distance, the other twitching as it strained to follow. She might have been talking to herself, each short phrase drowned in a sea of silence.

'I said about you, but he wouldn't have it. He hit me. We've been arguing anyway. He won't tell me what it is. That's how this happened.' She touched the skin around her bruised eye carefully, exploring the sensation.

'Come off it. I've got his number,' said H. Jo ignored this.

'Would you get me some coffee,' she said, then, after a moment, 'please.'

H didn't move.

'I haven't come to get you cups of coffee,' he said. 'I haven't come to *do* anything. I've come in case, this time – you want to come. Matter of choice . . . but yes, you look awful, I'll get you some.'

Jo glanced at me rapidly, then looked away again.

'Such a son,' she said as soon as H was too far away to

hear. 'I'm not blind, you know. I can see it must look as if we ought to be the other way round. It looks like I'm out of control. But you'd think differently if you really knew about us.' I nodded, unable to take my eyes off her spoiled face. 'His father was a marvellous man, died young, Accidental.'

'How terrible,' I murmured in the pause she left for me.

'He's gone his own way. I go mine, or try to.'

H returned, set the cup down in front of Jo. We sat in silence until he shrugged his shoulders and said, 'I'll be leaving at six tomorrow morning, with the tide. You can come with me, it's up to you.' He spoke in a toneless, hopeless voice, as if he wished his words to be lost before they were heard. Jo looked down at her silver painted nails, scratching at rust blisters on the table top.

'I just might,' she mumbled without conviction, 'I just might.' She threw back her hair; it was brittle, its artificial waves shone like metal in the sun. She must have been about forty-five, poised right on the edge of real age, but there was something about her at that moment that made such calculations irrelevant. The disquiet and pity I'd felt vanished. She closed her eyes and offered her face up to the blazing sky. H was staring at Jo too, and we both looked away as she opened her eyes again.

'But you know me, Haley. I probably won't.' She drank her coffee. Her hand was shaking, but she spilled none. 'Thanks. I'll get some sleep now –' She turned to me and held out her hand. Already the cream on her face had dried to a powdery film several shades lighter than the surrounding skin; the bruises showed through like damp under whitewash. She walked away with small determined steps, her back straight. She didn't look back. H didn't watch her go.

The sun had burnt away both shadows and dew, the temperature began to soar. I pushed back my chair and stretched. The island's spell had loosened its grip. I felt free, or that I might be. Every inch of me felt different, as if charged, vivid. I turned to speak to H. I can't remember what I was going to say, for at that moment, my breath ready, vocal chords pitched, there was a faint click; I saw blackness spread in the eye of a lens, then disappear in a fraction of a second. H wound on the film. He stood up, hung the camera over his shoulder and held out his hand.

'I shall be going at six tomorrow morning, with the tide,' he repeated. Again, the unusual balance he gave to his words and the spaces between made it difficult to tell whether this was his way of saying that we would not meet again, or a neutral statement of fact, or an invitation. But he had my picture in the black and silver box. I nodded. He turned and left, brushing against me as he squeezed between two chairs. I stayed sitting, unable to move. Looking back, I see that I was afraid.

The main subjects of H's photographs were his mother, Jo, and the moments just before her arrival, waiting for her.

There is one of Jo walking down Island Paradise Long Beach, shortly after I had passed her and the man on my way back to Kim. She is walking towards H; the picture was taken the moment before she changed direction, turning sharply back to land instead of continuing to meet H. Though distant, she is in sharp focus; her eyes are screwed against the sun, her expression is querulous and uncertain. She is looking straight into the camera, but does not seem to see it. Much further back, on the very edge of the picture, is another figure; it must be the man, walking towards the sea. And my footprints are visible in the foreground, but I am not there.

In another, taken from the side, Jo is alone, or seems to be. She is sitting upright on the beach. Her skin looks very white against the sand. Her eyes are downcast, she's studying her hands, which lie upturned on her thighs. Her hands are very small, plump and unlined. The broad curve of her shoulder is highlighted, oiled and catching the full glare of the sun. Her breasts hang, mostly hidden by her arm, but I can see that the nipples scarcely protrude and the aureoles look swollen, almost painful. In this picture Jo looks both old and young, contained, yet at the same time spillable; it was taken the first day H visited Island Paradise.

There is one, taken very close, of Jo talking. I can't see to whom, but guess it was the man with glasses. Her whole face is concentrated, her gaze focussed with unsettling intensity just to my left as I look. Her lips are pulled together and pout slightly as if she was about to make the sound 'p': '*Please*' I imagine her saying. I can see lines on her face, the gently downwards pull of cheeks, lips and chin; her eyes, large and slightly protuberant, are watering; she may even be crying.

There are others. In none of them does she look knowingly into the camera. None is posed, none, I suspect, voluntary. I met Jo only once, and these images I have are filtered through H's eyes. H still says that it is too easy to pity Jo, though oddly enough it is when looking at these photographs he took that I do.

In the afternoon I lay alone in the green glow of the tent. Outside, someone was laughing. It was Jo. I heard the man's voice, low. Her laughter continued, soft and melting as little curls of butter. The new tent must be theirs. I knew she wouldn't go in the morning. Go where? Where was it that H could take her, *me*, on a virtually unlimited travel pass? *Take me away*, I thought. Jo and the man were zipped up in their new blue tent. Perhaps they were laughing together at H, who was alone, who'd offered to take Jo away from her half-age lover, who'd hit her, who wouldn't tell and wouldn't listen. Perhaps the battle between them felt different now, perhaps the thought of H lay between them as they moved together, hurting, hating. What would happen? Why was I thinking this? It was not something within my knowledge or experience. *Something's wrong. Take me away.* I sat up. My skin glowed white in the green light. They were silent now. I crouched to fasten my shoe, photocards spilled out of my shirt pocket, my smooth young face on each; I left them where they fell and pushed through the flaps into the air outside. I could no longer bear to be Laurie Hunter. I ached from it, I wanted something different; I wanted to escape, and the man with the camera, H, with his fierce concentration and even speech seemed my only hope.

That night Kim and I returned late from the bar. The tents were unearthly in darkness, some reflecting just enough light to be visible as pieces of colourless density in the air, others, lit from within, glowed and flickered, luminous. *They are space ships come to take me away*, I thought; *we are under water but I am not drowning, I can see in the dark and breathe even beneath the sea, if only I get a chance to try.* Kim stumbled over a guy rope; he was drunk, breathing heavily and grasping my arm for support from time to time.

'I love Island Paradise,' he said, his eyes tight shut in the darker than darkness inside the tent, the canvas bag that swaddled us together, kept out the rain that never would come. He lay on his back. 'And I love you. It's a good life we lead, isn't it? When I was a child it was different. There was something in the air all the time – fear? – I always felt uneasy – whatever it was, it's gone now, hasn't it, Laurie?'

'All gone, Kim,' I answered.

'All gone,' he continued. 'Children grow up. No nightmares. Everything gets better over time . . . simple really. . . . Why don't you want a baby, Laurie? . . . I wish . . .'

I held Kim's hand as he drifted into sleep, waited.

It was just light, the last traces of drizzle in the air, the sky mottled pale-yellow, grey, white. The tents billowed and shrank, soft shapes in a breath of wind. It was as if the world would fade away if I tried to touch it.

I didn't kiss Kim gently before I left, didn't turn to mouth a soft silent goodbye to all I'd known before; I left no message, but dressed outside in my stoutest clothes and slipped away, desperate, running. I paused at the clifftop, looking down. Far below, the sea was covered by a layer of mist; the breaking of waves was dampened and distant. I took off my shoes. I threw down my sunhat and bag; they disappeared without a sound. Spray hung in the air; the world was weightless, I parted it and brushed it aside like a curtain of cobwebs. *Mustn't be late*, I left my shoes perched side by side like pair of stupid birds, *if he's not there, if he didn't mean me to come?* I ran; wave by wave the tide was rising around the edges of the island.

H sat hunched in a dingy hitched to one of the bollards on the pier. He had the oars pulled up and across to make a ledge to rest his arms on. He smiled.

'I was just about to go,' he said.

'Can I come?' I asked.

'Of course,' he said coolly, 'if you want.' The dingy rocked ferociously as I climbed in. We looked at each other.

'You look sad,' I said.

'A little. On the other hand, you look very happy. You've been running again. Every time I see you, you're running.'

'What about your mother?' H was already pulling us through calm grey water that was just beginning to speckle with gold. It was odd to see someone do that for real, not just exercise. I knew then that I had been right: we were going somewhere else, with no thought of return. He paused, looking at the oars, held high and dripping back into the sea.

'Jo? She isn't coming. Never would. Look, that's *Bird*,' he gestured with his oar to a small yacht anchored at the very edge of the harbour, straining and lurching in currents that sped through a narrow channel of deeper water. It looked very small and unstable, the rigging whipping even in the lightest of breezes. I'd never been on a boat before.

'I'm a disappeared person now,' I said. 'Surveillance will be looking for me soon, or my body. I threw some clothes over the cliff. I want to just disappear. I don't want to go back –'

He interrupted: 'Perhaps they'll be searching for me as well –' and turned to look at me as he spoke, the pupils of his eyes small in the growing light.

'I killed someone this morning,' he said, then turned away, and both oars bit the water together, pulling us away from Island Paradise, dip, scull, dip, scull, as if nothing had been said.

The Journey

The days are whisper quiet; each side of the announcements, morning and afternoon, the streets all but empty. You can make out figures behind the glass in some of the older buildings; now and then a messenger carrying a parcel waits at a crossing, a delivery is unloaded. Paper mainly, here. Ringed by stumpy hills, as far from the sea as it could possibly be, Central City's becoming the main site of administration and exchange. Very quiet and clean. Everyone works. They work in the Central Registry of Citizens, the Allocations office, Contracts and so on. Links with Rocket, far to the north, are growing stronger. I've not been there since I went on a tour as a child, but we see it often enough on the announcements: a familiar long-shot, that approach to the Council chambers. They're surrounded on all sides by water, a vast pearly lake reflecting the sky. The trafficway cuts straight across to the main façade of gleaming emblems. Glimpsed through faceted glass, the towering indoor garden, moist, luxuriant, and the last tombs to be built: Briggs, Karancheck, Minito and Ellulah, sheathed in lead, covered in stone, engraved with gold.

The plains cities aren't on the whole so well built as Rocket or Central. They deal in heavy components, food processes, seem to grow and shrink unpredictably, lack the strong plain surfaces, the mature trees, the sense of permanence that you get with administration. There are exceptions: Dove City, where I grew up and then lived with Kim; it was components there, but a beautiful place because of the river.

In the thick daytime hush, everyone is working. I used to, but am no longer productive. No right, wrong, click! I'm not part of progress any more. Going backwards fast. Down the chute, clunk, like H's empty bottles. . . .

I used to like my work. I took trouble. What for, I think, to make this? This damned silence, this apartment we don't use? Is it for this we've developed a technology to extract light and heat from Three, to make metals in the sky? To give me a choice of four kinds of bath? Is that what I'm supposed to pay the Price for? But then, in the blink of an eye it can all seem beautiful, as beautiful as any island paradise seen from above, though distinct. The clear lines of the buildings, the careful juxtaposition of muted colour with the bright flare of glass reflecting sky; the near-white pavement, the pink trafficway with its steel guardrails – a haze of light, a maze of stone, shining in sudden rain.

Lunchtime. The lifts descend, the doors open. Hair and cloth flapping in the wind. It's April. The crowd mills, divides, heading for the nearest screens. I can't just watch. I have to go.

The announcements are always in the past tense, vague, undifferentiated. On the other hand, we're encouraged to look to the future, and the announcements' regular punctuation of our day gives us a kind of sense of time moving on, not something you can properly measure but a rhythm that never stops, that leaves no room. When you're old, it feels different. Time draws to a point; the rhythm doesn't fit.

Today, which was windy and bright, so that clouds kept blowing over the sun causing brief periods of shadow, there was some real information. We learned that a hundred and twenty-six people have died Untimely on Three, due to multiple failures of equipment; someone's not doing their testing very well, I thought.

'*In the light of this terrible tragedy,*' said the announcer, '*we must take stock of our safety procedures.*'

Someone will be demoted, I thought. The wind kept

blowing bits of hair out of my hat and into my eyes. An Accidental Death is almost as bad as one Wilfully Inflicted.

One hundred and twenty-six. A huge and exact figure. Gathered round the telescreen, we looked at each other aghast. It must have happened about a week ago, I thought, but for all I know it could be years. A list of names was read out, and an hour's remembrance was announced, for the duration of which all screens held a picture of Three, and everyone sat quietly and watched it.

> The only struggle is the struggle for improvement, for resources, between us and the huge outside.

You would never guess that Three was worth anyone dying for. A battered, dry-looking planet, but apparently the richest energy source yet to be exploited off One (each has been better than the one before). We'll need it in a few years' time, we'll need it badly.

> The search for power costs us ingenuity and dedication, but it must not cost us Life.

Why not life? I thought jeeringly, maybe that's the Price. Maybe they're paying it like I have to. But I kept my face suitably solemn.

The struggle for Power used to excite me. I understood that off-earth exploitation had made us free, as much as the Treaty itself. As a child, of course, I used to follow our progress on charts that I designed myself: size of population; expected increase of demand; power needed; power actual, potential. Childishly, I played at prediction, assuming that it was the demand that came first and that the struggle was to meet it. (Sometimes now, I wonder if it is the other way round, and the demand, that is the size and expectations – the lifespan even – of the population, is shaped to fit the supply.) I was taken to see one of the crews return, and cheered until my throat hurt. Our heroes. I felt they had done it for me. And I remember there was a model of Two that came free with breakfast foods. You collected the platforms and operatives and fixed them on, week by week, with glue, as it happened.

And later, I tried to understand the technical manoeuvres involved in extraction, conversion, transmission and off-space use. I went on a course, but people working in these prestigious fields are off-puttingly superior and precious about their job (they called it a *vocation*) and I left before the end.

Now, I don't care. I don't care about the tragedy, and I don't care about the celebrations which take place every time part of the construction process is successfully completed. A half-holiday is announced. People dress up and wander the streets in large groups, singing and chanting slogans from Energy Corporation advertisements. *So long as the Power lasts* – I did it once, my throat raw, my fist clenched. . . . Their voices start in heavy unison, then break hopelessly apart. Bottles and windows are smashed. Surveillance turn a blind eye; it's always over by the morning. *So long as the Power lasts.*

I find myself thinking: but I didn't know any of this hundred and twenty-six. Three is difficult; so what, I'll probably be dead, Timely or not, before the Power runs out. . . . If anything, I feel almost elated because something's gone wrong. Is this a symptom of age? If so, could it be why we're not wanted, because we say *I don't care* of the only struggle that remains? On the other hand, perhaps I would care if I wasn't being pushed out of it. If I hadn't been to Island Paradise, and come back.

'The old have too much time on their hands,' says H, pointedly. Sometimes I think he means it.

'You don't know what it's like!' I say. 'Being crossed out. Waiting.' Pro: he makes my meals, and never raises his voice. Con: he won't talk about the past, our past. He won't even listen about it. Would I follow him now, as I did then?

'Look,' he says, his voice soft and eager, almost like Kim's when I'd cried and he'd suggested a holiday, 'why don't we do it our way? That's the best that we can do. There's a little light by the window . . .'

'Not yet,' I say between clenched teeth.

'Afraid?'

'No.'

But sometimes I am. Sometimes I'm afraid and think, what would he do if I told him no, never; or even if I simply keep on saying no, not yet?

I suppose I should be glad I've got someone, anyone. I can just about imagine being on my own, but I can't imagine being with anyone other than H.

As the island dwindled behind us, the sea grew variegated, turquoise and cobalt. There was a strong swell, the water stretching itself into great troughs, rolling upwards, curving over but never breaking into foam. I didn't know where we were going. I could remember the shape of Island Paradise on the map, a rough triangle drawn with a shaking hand, but where was the nearest piece of land? I didn't know, I remembered it only in isolation.

I was in a boat with H and he had killed someone; the most surprising thing of many is that I didn't jump into the sea and swim straight back. If I'd been at home, the word itself would have made me flinch and gag. Killing. A cold, hard word that doesn't judge. A blunt fact, not a crime. Killing's not the same as Wilfully Inflicted Untimely Death, which does not exist, is illegal, unheard of, unspeakable. *We have bowed our heads and turned away from slaughter*.

But we weren't at home; far from it, and getting farther. H steered us on through the empty sea. I didn't try to swim away. I didn't ask him any questions. I wasn't even afraid of him. The ugly word hung, understood but somehow unassimilated. I didn't quite know what it meant. I lay back and felt the motion of the waves, the shudder of their parting, the straining of the sail.

On and on we went, not speaking, each alone with whatever we thought. The sea grew gradually rougher. *Bird* lifted high by the swell, seemed to hang suspended above the rest of the sea. *He might kill me*, I thought suddenly. The boat plummeted down, only to be borne up again at the moment of impact. I knew he wouldn't.

On all sides the horizon was an indistinct muddle of pale-blue mists and clouds; the island had gone. *Have you seen her?* Kim would be asking, his smooth forehead bunched tight with perplexity and confusion; light-brown hair and hazel eyes, a sunhat with a brim, walks slowly, asks sudden questions then subsides into silence, doesn't want children, works in light tech, sleeps without dreaming, takes her physical pleasure from me, now and then from others, lightly, no signs of distress, wanted so much to come, her idea, I can't understand. They would find my shoes on top of the cliff. They would start looking in the sea, and perhaps that was where I would indeed end up. Who was it H had killed? The man with glasses? Jo? Someone else entirely? – And if I lived, I thought, one day I would have to go back, or we would be found, then it would be impossible to explain. *What had I done*? And I could not believe that I was there, with him.

H had fastened the tiller and sat, waiting for me to look up. The wind blew hard and steady. I was crouched beneath the sail.

'Are you frightened of me?' he shouted above the wind and the slicing spray. I shook my head.

No, because I don't believe it, I thought with sudden relief; he sat so loosely, his elbows resting on his knees, his hands hanging between them; he couldn't have. He reached to open the locker beside him, and took something out. It was small and seemed to be made of white plastic. It didn't look real. He stood and threw it in a huge hurtling arc out to sea.

'You're safe,' he said, opening his hands as he moved carefully nearer to me, 'it will sink like a stone.'

'That's not a gun,' I said. 'This morning? When? I didn't sleep. I heard nothing. It's a lie.'

'You wouldn't have,' he smiled. 'It's not a gun in a film, it's modern, and very quiet. It uses air.' He paused, waiting for me to ask – and then suddenly I believed it. I imagined him crouching, as I had seen him do with his camera, utterly still, waiting for that moment when the subject reached its greatest eloquence. Then – a single shot, air. I imagined it, I still didn't know what it meant, but my pulse fluttered and throbbed. I turned away and looked at the sea.

'Such things exist, you know,' he said softly. 'I bought it from one of my customers. It's what Surveillance have.'

'Surveillance don't carry weapons –'

'Yes they do.'

On Paradise Island, Kim sat all day in the beach café, waiting for me. I can imagine him, patiently watching the televideo as the announcements come and go, but looking away to check each time a shadow falls across the table. When at last he sits alone in a pool of shade, they begin to take down the striped umbrellas, and reluctant but still hopeful he goes to report to Surveillance, who have already found my bag, full of waterlogged identification, cottonwool and so on. A search is instituted. I sometimes get moody and tired, he says. Perhaps I was walking alone, rested, and forgot my things on the beach. Perhaps I was in the forest – perhaps Kim even went to look, hurrying along the criss-cross paths, calling my name into the emerald shadow, the rustling leaves.

I who caused all this had escaped. It was dusk. The sea slapped and sighed all around us. I saw the first star, then thousands, in a deep violet sky edged with gold. We drifted. It grew completely dark, and the water sounds seemed yet louder and more alive. There was no one, nothing else, anywhere. I ceased to think and remember, I lay rocked by the water that was drowning who I had been, carrying me away. I felt part of the space around us. H's face was close in the dark. I felt his warmth. My breath caught and altered. We were closer. The sense of almost-touch became a kiss. We exhaled slowly, touching the world, breaking the surface to breathe. A second's respite, then again, that precise moment, again; each touch entailing the next, now this, then this, *now, again*, agreement, persuasion moving with the rise and fall of the surrounding water. Again. I was away from the island, slipping further and further away into scale without boundaries, my eyes in long focus in darkness and all around the humming, sighing, pause and breath, pause, and breath, pause, come and go of the sea. Two strangers upside down and inside out, taken softly apart and put together, quickening at the contact of skin, *again, again*, escaped.

I held H tightly. I could see the shape of his face, upturned, heard him moisten his lips before he spoke: I put my hand over his mouth. I didn't want to know, not then; I didn't want the blunt clumsiness of words after the dumb subtlety of touch. I wanted to stay as we were. We drifted in dark, in and out of sleep. The sea was phosphorescent, the sky was black, we lay between.

I wept. The way we'd touched each other was like something I remembered, although it had never felt that way before. That quality of excitement and bewilderment at the same time, of confusion, and danger and soft consolation, there, on the water. . . . I suppose I could weep all over again, because it's never been the same again, never so good. Just once. In that sense our relationship's hardly been at all. It's not sex that makes him come home each night, that makes me listen for the lift, his footsteps, hand on the latch. It's not that. And as for the rest, I often say to myself, I'm going, I'm going to take myself to the lift and never come back; but I never have. I've no one else. We got ourselves in so deep, neither of us can have anyone else. I've not the time in any case.

We lay in each other's arms. The first segment of sun nudged above the sea and the texture of the water began to show, our hands and faces shone, and then there were streaks and swathes of red as the sun, flickering in its own brilliance, inched up, concentrating shape and light into a deep yellow and dazzlingly perfect circle. Still the sky changed: from white to gold to blue, second by second transforming into day.

'It was Jo,' he said loudly and deliberately, without preamble. I wish he never had. I wish that now, now that I have a picture of Jo alive and mouthing please, glowing in the faint light of the screen, now that I can feel the weight of it.

'They'll probably think,' I said then, 'that I did it.' It was still difficult for me to use the word, but I accepted the information in passing; I took it, as if it was something I'd always known and temporarily forgotten. I took it like a coat to wrap around my shoulders. Like an offered drink. Something difficult to give back. I laughed. I didn't think about paying prices. I thought instead that it was possible we were the perfect pair of escapees: how it could be said that on Island Paradise, a woman with hazel eyes and no dreams went mad and killed someone, her motive and means immaterial because, acknowledging both transgression and penalty, she killed herself.

'Perhaps. If they do, we're probably safe.'

On Island Paradise, in the slow, dry, golden afternoon of the day after our departure, a small boy opens Jo's tent and spends half an hour playing with her golden hair. Later he returns, bringing two of his friends. One of them screams, a glass-shattering wail, not loud but painfully high. Jo is cold and stiff. Flies have gathered round her head. Parents emerge and begin running round the tents, opening their flaps at random, trying to locate the alarm. The air fills with the rip of fasteners torn open, and the scream sings on.

And they find her, hastily cover her up. Jo's young man is arrested, but he has an alibi, having spent the night talking and drinking with someone else.

Flights from the island are suspended until the killer and the weapon are found. If nothing is allowed to leave the island, then, given time, the killer will be found. The holiday-makers assent. It is far better, thinks the director of Holiday Flights (Paradise), in her cool office hidden from view, that they return with tales of a mystery solved, a tragedy over and explained. That way, the story will be shorter, and more easily forgotten.

People sit upright on the beach, their eyes wide open and focussed on the shore. Walking home, no one strays from the paths.

The planes stand silent on the airstrip, and every hour more holiday-makers, growing increasingly restless, come to look at them, and to ask the authorities what progress has been made, and when they will be able to go home. Their holiday had been spoiled. They sit in the airport and drink. The beaches grow emptier. One by one, everyone is being questioned. No one knows or heard anything. And no one wants to sleep in the tents any more. They take their mats and quilts to the airport lounge. An adolescent girl throws a beer glass at the back of her father's head, then runs across the tarmac to the planes.

'Take me away from here,' she shouts, 'take me away.'

'So where d'you wanna go?' asks the bartender, catching her in his arms, laughing. He spins her round and round, staggers. He's drunk again; she breaks free and runs back the way she came.

*

H lay with obvious pleasure in the frail boat in the midst of unending sea. Our arms touched. My mind was blank. I did not want to know anything else, I was satisfied, I was happy. Hours passed. We sped through the sea, casting up spray. The wind was hot, a powder of salt grew on our skins; we sipped warm water from white mugs. H talked.

'I killed someone once before, by accident. My father, in fact. When I was a child. I was playing with a Power line he was fixing. He died instantly. His skin looked like caked soot and came off when it was touched. They hurried me away and said it was not my fault. I was screaming sorry, sorry. Jo said it was not my fault. There was a full Accident Inquiry, lasting nearly a week. They said it wasn't my fault. The day after, however, my throat hurt and I couldn't speak. The movements of my lips and throat, the rhythms of listening and response – everything had gone, though I still understood what other people said: they said it was not my fault. I had to learn speech again, slowly, as you might learn to swim or dance.' His hands were full of rope, slowly prising the sodden knots apart.

'It was learned differently the second time. With effort. And I'm changed.' He looked up briefly, then turned back to his work. The words came slowly, one by one.

'I don't remember him alive at all,' he continued, speaking to the sea, which rolled unceasingly towards us, as if pouring over the edge of the world. 'You can guess what it was like after.'

'I can't,' I said. 'Nothing like that has ever happened to me. I played with my music machine and went to school. I met Kim and went to work. I came on holiday. Now perhaps I've gone mad.'

'Of course you can imagine,' he said. 'I've no loyalty. Sometimes I think the whole world' – he gestured at it – 'is a thin skin you could burst, just like that. There's a feeling of something rushing away, fast. You know what I mean, don't you?' Quietly, he began laughing. I was not afraid. I knew what he meant. Perhaps we were both mad. Are. Perhaps not. Soon it was night again, our second, violet, transfixed with stars. We ate biscuits, drank more water, and while I slept, H steered on.

Dawn on Paradise Island: I see the bartender walking on the runway, arm in arm with a young woman, a faint smile breaking through the tears drying on her face.

'I'm innocent,' she says. 'It's obvious, ordinary people don't do things like that.'

'But we're all ordinary,' he says. 'Doesn't work, does it?' The smoked glass of the lounge looks like tarnished brass, their silhouettes walk across it. She pulls her arm away.

'Sorry –' she says, and strides back to the lounge. They are being watched from the flight control tower. The simplest and best thing, thinks the director of Holiday Flights, would be just to pick someone out and ship them off. The thought shocks her; she rationalizes: this isn't doing anyone any good.

Stella's mother Karen weeps. Their surname, Artel, has put the family at the top of the list: they are the first to be questioned twice, and they'll be first again the third time round. Her husband in one office, she and Stella next door. Her hair keeps falling in her eyes. It's hot, so hot. They haven't even had breakfast. She feels singled out. She holds Stella's hand tightly in hers, but the tighter, the wetter, it pulls and squirms, slips repeatedly away.

'Sit still,' she says, smiling bravely at the two Surveillance officers. 'I wish I could help, it's such a terrible, terrible thing. But there's nothing. We were fast asleep, weren't we, Stell?'

'Your tent – cream?'

'Yes. With a blue pennant.'

'It was in the adjacent row; surely you might have seen – heard –'

'Sound travels easy through cloth, Mrs Artel,' says the other officer, '*think*.'

It's as if he'd said not think, but imagine. Yes. Perhaps she saw a figure crawling between the tents, heard the thump of a heart, two hearts, one, alone, faster.

'No,' she says. Suddenly she's convinced it was her husband. Then no, she thinks, it was me, it was –

'I did it,' says Stella, her eyes aghast, her voice hot with excitement. For a second Karen believes her.

'With my stick,' she continues. 'I stuck it in her.'

'You did not,' Karen shrieks, roughly grabbing Stella's arm. 'She didn't!'

'Let go of me, you're hurting.'

Weary, Surveillance part them. The number of confessions, all improbable, is mounting. If only there hadn't been so many witnesses to the discovery of the body. . . .

'Sorry,' says Karen. It's heartfelt: she feels broken, shamed.

I was alone in the edgeless sea, with a quiet, twice-learned voice and small neat hands that had killed twice – father, *Accidental*; mother, *Wilful* – and escaped, and held me in the night. I was tired, happy. The sun, the creaking of ropes, the straining sail, almost unbearably vivid.

'What was it like afterwards?' I asked.

'Good and bad. I've no intention of doing it again.'

'It's wrong to – kill,' I said. It was hard to say the word, but I felt lighter afterwards.

'I'll take you back to Island Paradise, now, if you wish.' He raised his hand as if to do so.

His movements were gentle, contained, yet confident. He smiled as he spoke of the most terrible things, and made them less important. He was a mystery. He seemed to know where we were going, and I'd followed him. The sea took and lost a thousand shapes with every passing second. Fish leapt in clean curves out of the water amid a whirr of fins. Droplets of water caught the sun in sudden rainbows.

'No,' I said, 'I don't want to go back.'

Tomorrow is Remembrance Day. Sorry Day, it's sometimes called. I'm not looking forward to it, and shouldn't think anyone does. We fast. No one goes to work. There are no announcements. We will wear black armbands, and all morning and all afternoon, accounts of atrocities and wars in Time Before will boom from large loudspeakers outside. No escape from it: gassings, mutilations, genocide, large and small wars, bleeding eyes, skins falling off, charred shadows, acts of revenge, sexual murder, assassination, torture, starvation, abortion, described in careful detail and in a soft, slightly pained voice. We will weep and vomit and try to plug our ears. We will all burn with pain, with guilt, as we stand hours later in front of the blank telescreen, and at six o'clock we'll shout, three times, all together: 'Deliver us. Deliver us. Deliver us.' And there'll be a few seconds agonizing silence before words come in answer. 'We are sorry.'

'Sorry,' we intone with relief. 'Oh, sorry.'

'We have bowed our heads and turned away from slaughter.'

'Away from slaughter.'

'Wilfully Inflicted and Untimely Death cannot but be forbidden.'

'Forbidden, forbidden.'

'In this our epoch we shall for the first time adhere to natural prohibition. It's over. We're free.'

'We're free!'

The words echo, subside, become the babble of celebration. And there will be lightshows, music and dancing, and people will be stirred to kiss and embrace and make love. More than half of all children born are conceived on Remembrance Day. Our pledge for the future. But H and I will go home early, slipping through the red-faced crowds of revellers. We'll know we're different, and feel lonely. We've both wanted to kill, he has; we're still here to remind each other of it. On Remembrance Day, we often argue, with unusual bitterness.

'You started it all,' I'll say. 'I was just like everyone else before I met you. I was getting on fine. I was happy.'

'I didn't force you to come,' he'll reply, 'far from it.'

I look at him now, sleeping, and I am neither happy nor unhappy, but I'm not satisfied. I sit by the window at night, each night, think over the day's announcements and make this account of our lives. H and I will come to an end, and what is outside and beyond, the steady pulse of Power in cables, the quiet manoeuvrings of Surveillance, the dark ships moving through dappled seas, the stored weaponry, that awful legacy of Time Before, chemical, nuclear, biological, waiting for its miracle, the rockets delving into space: they will not end. We will not see it.

I think how the world changed so very rapidly after the Unfought War, saved at the last minute of the last hour. The killing stopped. It must have been beautiful, as the woman with the long hair, bronze or blonde or black, always says. It must have been as if people woke up and found themselves elsewhere, as if deep snow had fallen in the night. The aggressors became as one. Peace. There would be no more bodies on the ground. None. No more Untimely Death. The peoples of the world shuddered with relief. It's difficult to imagine. It's difficult, almost, to believe. All the things we take for granted were once not there, or were different.

H's body, though scarred, is still small and neat, defies gravity. My flesh has slipped gently down its frame of bone, I feel it settling about me when I lie down, I feel it slipping away. I'm tired of it often; I want to climb out, I want to be a skeleton filled and surrounded with fine warm golden sand.

Yes, one thing I do want: my own particular end. I don't want to pay any price; I don't want any dream of mine to come true.

The Archipelago

Yesterday, a new secretary of the International Council, Vincent, took office. He has flaming red hair. The previous one, Speedwell, died, not Timely, from *unexpected* medical causes. We saw a bit of the ceremony; taking the rocket in one hand and the dove in the other, he declared:

> My work is to preserve what has been gained,

and swore:

> I will strive to maintain and to facilitate the aims and aspirations set out in the International Force's Treaty. I will endeavour to relate the proceedings of the International Council promptly and accurately to the population.

And, we were told, new personnel, highly qualified, have set off for Three. Even accounting for the Untimely Dead, it must be a crowded planet. The construction deadline will still be met, despite setbacks. The crime rate's as low as ever. The birth rate's slightly down. . . . I took the lift, feeling it pressing upwards on my feet. There were half a dozen homeworkers coming up as well. Two of the women talked.

'Your father still living with you?' one said. The other nodded. 'Never mind. Can't be long.'

'Can't be too soon. We haven't had a holiday for two years. Can't take him, can't leave him. Can't afford it now anyway. The rent's going up already.' She was on the verge of tears. The other leaned over, touching her friend on the shoulder, and began whispering in her ear. Their faces became carefully empty. *Plotting*, I thought. But also, I could see her point of view. Biting my lip, I watched them in the mirror, and missed my floor. All of a sudden, everyone's wearing shades of green. I'm still in grey and lilac.

'Can't be too soon.' At least H won't say that of me. One way of looking at what he did to Jo is that he just did it a bit early, and more straightforwardly. Another thing is that he saved her from paying a Price she herself never agreed to. Of course, he only did that by making her pay another, but she didn't know. It strikes me that each generation ought to be asked about a thing like that, instead of it becoming habit, nature, because once that's happened no one even considers choosing. Or asking, for example, do we have to have a Price at all?

I think the woman in the lift, young, green-clad, grey-eyed, mild-faced, wants to kill her father. He's in her way. He costs her. That's one thing, one kind of killing; similarly, I think it possible that someone killed our old secretary Speedwell. Maybe many people want to kill, even though they can't pronounce the word, even though it's illegal, unheard of and unspeakable, even though they don't do it. And maybe other people have morbid fantasies like H and I do, whisper to each other. 'There's a little light by the window . . .', answer 'Not yet . . .', dig their fingernails in that bit too hard. And I can guess a killing, even imaginary, is a place where the perpetrator's head breaks through into pure air, as after a long and stifling dive. The relief. Nothing before has felt so real. The body on the ground, the fragments of a broken law: and an implication: if we haven't got what we were promised, and I've proved it, then maybe we don't have to pay the Price. . . . Maybe everyone dreams now and then their own kind of killing. *I wish you were dead.* Sorry. Sorry. The progression from thought, to speech, to act.

Perhaps when people get close, that is, closer than most people do, than Kim and I ever did, to something, to each other: there's something wrong and we blame each other for it. There's something we want to find out and we tear each other apart looking, in the wrong place. We look inside instead of out, because it's more manageable. Or, we look in the other person instead of ourselves, where hidden at the bottom of the lake of oil we ourselves have hidden the answer. Speedwell. Someone's father, old like me. In the way. Jo. I think Kay next door killed her murmuring lover; anyway, he died Untimely and she was gone when Surveillance arrived. I don't know where she is now. Perhaps escaped. There was no publicity, but that might be because no one saw. I am convinced, I *know*, there is more violence than we are told about. Arguments, with no apology. Often I hear sounds like fighting in the streets. I look out, and it's gone.

It seems as if the world hangs suspended in peace, like a goldfish suffocating in its bowl, and secretly, ashamedly, in darkness, people are beginning to fight. I'm not sure why. I guess. These events are not broadcast but I hear them in smothered screams, deduce them from disappearances. I may be wrong. I'm sick. I don't like it, but I feel excited, especially at night. It feels like the only place to go. It feels out of control. It feels real, night.

I'm not sure why, but I think – I think it's a message, a kind of truth, because –

'You're avoiding the real issue,' says H, H for hypocrite, slurring his words, jabbing his finger in the air. These days he's drinking far too much. If cigarettes were still around he'd be smoking too much as well. 'Which is: what are you going to do when you have to have your appointment at Age Counselling, which you can't avoid.

What good's all this memory and speculation then, what good? What am I going to do if –?'

'Shut up!' I say. 'Leave me alone.'

He shrugs. 'Look. There's only two choices, they'll do it for you or you'll do it yourself, our way.'

'What about an Accident?' Suddenly, we both laugh, folding, clutching at each other. There aren't many times like that. After, we sit, weak and breathless, daring each other to start again. I like his laugh. It's not like the way he speaks, which is often hard and still strange. It lights me up inside, chases away stiffness, makes my face feel clean and warm.

Our way ahead was strewn with islands, many of them embedded in patches of mirror-flat water. Leaves and pieces of waterlogged timber floated by. The air smelled of trees and damp soil; the colours deepened. We were going to land. Wind came from all directions, filling, then slapping and puckering the sails; boom and ropes swung confused. Some of the islands seemed to race erratically towards us, others dwindled and disappeared. Our chosen island was behind us now. With the sail, fighting every inch, finally down and lashed, H turned us over to Power. We shook and exploded into noise, swung round. The smell of hot lubricating oil overlaid that of the land. I steered; the tiller transmitted watery forces below, doubling, redoubling, proliferating, and vibrated in my hand. A steady wake parted either side of us, and the staccato beat of the engine was music after hearing so long only the edgeless sounds of sea and wind. We accelerated, the pitch of the engine coming thinner, its rhythm more insistent. The wind we made combed through us; we had to shout against it. My eyes were fixed on the patch of sand ahead, small but growing, growing; I wanted to never stop –

H cut the engine and in the abrupt silence, the strangeness of slowing down, I picked up the camera and took his photograph with our island as background. His eyes are shut in the picture, his hands fluttering about his face – I have it on the table now. It's blurred and over-lit – he's about to laugh, like we just were. My lungs still stretch from it, my face is still tight. But we were at the beginning then, in open sea. Water. Now it's near the end, a room, night. I wish I could go. I wish I could be shot into the stars. All those years ago I tried to escape, and now I'm trapped. So's he, but he doesn't seem to care. Him, the room, the city. Me. Time narrowing to a point – night. Water.

And so we laughed as we waded through warm sea to our island, where the sound of the waves was carefree talk, and the clouds made dissolving pictures minute by minute in the sky. I remember the feeling I had there of always having words at the tip of my tongue – like freedom, like love, even paradise; words which superstition forbade me to utter, but which tasted sharply sweet in any case.

The water seemed friendly as my own blood. We dived. We swam deeper and deeper until we touched the seabed, where feathery plants swayed back and forth, and looking up, the blue there called out for a name of its own, absolutely particular. Tiny bubbles burst on the insides of our legs. We surfaced gradually, feeling the strong elongation of our bodies, their steady silent propulsion. We swam to meet each other, our skin glowing palely, foreshortened, our faces wet and childish.

H made the world literally different, and simple; even if, later, he took it away, I'm glad it happened, and anyway, as he says, it can't be undone. But was it him? Jo paid, didn't she? I try to add it up: was it worth it, to end up here? Is it bearable? Is this another Price?

Photographs. Island Paradise, H, Jo, the man, me. Our

journey: in the day, what I think I hear – and what I remember – at night seems impossible. Midday, the exodus from workplaces to watch the announcements, and after, people sit a while in squares, or order their shopping from telebooths. Sometimes I feel lonely. I'm lonely even when he comes home, often drunk. I get dressed when I hear the moan of the lift, and greet him at the door.

'You're drunk! Not again!' I say, complaining, but pleased he's back. Safe.

'Just up?' he replies, tit for tat. I pull him in.

'We should never have come back!' I wail sometimes, my voice like Jo's in the tent.

'Even so, we did,' he says, and puts his hand heavily on my shoulder. I'm shrinking. I used to be much taller than him. His breath smells sickly, synthetic.

'Lie on the bed?' he says, slurring slightly. 'There's a little light by the window.'

'Not yet,' I always say, although, if the day's been bad, I sometimes almost do. But that wasn't what we meant.

I'm afraid to say just 'No.' Afraid for him as much as me.

Escaped, H and I would sit opposite each other burrowing our feet into the coolness of wave-washed sand.

'I feel as if I have grown taller,' I'd say. 'Will this go on for ever? Will we grow tired of it?' Our toes met beneath the sand. 'Will it?' I'd repeat, 'will we?' reaching for him with my hands.

'Don't know,' he'd say, the waves and the wind lightening the severity of his enunciation, distracting me from the unsatisfactory nature of his answer, all his answers. Like the patterns made on sand by waves, his ribs rippled, hard but smooth beneath brown skin. The scattering of tiny hairs, the grain and pores and sweat-filled creases: I saw as if magnified the textures and patterns of his surfaces; my fingers pressed deep, wanting to know, unable, coming up against the hardness of bone. He seemed so permanent. I wanted to tear him apart.

'I love you,' I said.

'Jo was always saying that,' he replied, turning away.

The pressure of my fingers left marks on his shoulders, white then flooding dark. I thought of Jo, I still do, every time I bruise or see one.

Two or three times a day we would go for a swim. I never let him out of my sight. We caught fish, and collected dates. We slept. The sun rose and set, glorious; paradise.

'H,' I ask, 'what did you feel for me, all that time ago?'

'I can't remember. Why?' He yawns.

'I never thought about it at the time –' I say encouragingly, 'but –'

'Neither did I. Can't help.' He sits so still. Like a photograph of himself. Answers, but doesn't. It's as if he's not there, but he must be, because I hate him so much. He's a fact, not an explanation.

'You've got to help!' I shout, striding towards him, arm raised. He doesn't move. I don't do it; instead, I burst into tears.

'Get up early tomorrow,' H says, awkwardly kind. 'Keep a grip on yourself.'

'That's fine, coming from you.'

'Put your clothes on and come out with me. Spend the day at the theme park or something, and I'll meet you after work. We can get drunk, go and watch some pictures.'

I appreciate the concern, but no thanks. I've had enough of that: theme parks, amusements; slot the shuttle, join the stars. And the pictures: the last one I saw was a love story about a pale woman with green eyes and a slender man with curly hair. They both worked in a desert space base, they'd both been up more than once, performed well and earned more than most. They were OK for a baby. But then it turned out that he was infertile, and she would have to use insemination. However, the medical fees looked to be so high that she went off on her own and slept with a man with black hair and blue eyes, explaining to him why. The man with curly hair was mistrustful and upset. She was upset because he was upset. Blue eyes was concerned for both of them. They were in the kitchen, all together, weeping. They almost parted. The picture place was heaving with the sound of their sobs, and those of the audience. It's the end I remember really. They all go for a walk in the desert, at dusk. The first stars emerge. She points at them, smiling through her tears. They've all been up there. They've depended on each other for life. They've trusted each other. 'Oh, trust me,' she sighs to the one with curly hair. He looks into her eyes. We see the eyes, melting. We hear his voice: *Trust me*, he says: the title of the show. Together, they say 'Yes'. The screen went blank for a moment, and then we saw them from a long way above, the lovers hand in hand, and blue eyes walking jauntily back to the base; on the horizon an Explorer is launched. I saw that with Martina. I'm pretty sure I cried.

On Island Paradise, they were stranded: I see them sleeping in the airport lounge with the lights dimmed. Exhausted after days of fruitless interrogation, their foreheads are tight, their eyelids twitch and the children, waking often, whimper the questions that burrow their way into everyone's dreams:

What happened?

Haven't they caught him yet?
Why are we here?
Oh, when can we go home?

Home. Night. Water, the coming dust, sticking sour in nose and throat.

Dust

The weather, humid. This summer seems endless, baking, overcast. They say the world's stopped getting hotter, but it doesn't feel like it. I've just taken my second bath of the night. I don't bother to move about quietly when I get up. Now it's raining. It used to rain there, on our island, every night; great drops that slapped the skin and spread themselves generously across it, trickling behind and inside, collecting in crevices, falling again. Rain over sea is a richer, wilder sound than rain on land. I can hear it still. It comes and goes, oddly amplified by the shifting mass of water that waits to absorb it. We slept on the beach. I'd lie close to H, following him as he turned away in his sleep. When I touched his face, it was set, and the wetness tasted of salt. The different kinds of darkness dissolved into each other. I rolled out from the shelter we'd made with the dingy, out into the rain for relief.

The damp sand took a definite shape when pressed or scuffed, made a perfect print that could be felt and read even in the blind of night. Waking in the dark – ever since I've done it – it's like being a witness of something you're not meant to see. On Island Paradise, I'd woken in darkness to the sounds of splitting canvas and Jo's tear-pitched voice; curiosity, sleep, all blurred fragments. On our island without a name something surrounding me parted, slowly, continuously. I strained to see what was beyond. And now I sit, back here, tapping my fingers on noiseless keys, trying to bring back the past, hoping to break the future open. What's to come? I don't need to be there, just to know.

Each night, I longed for the sun to rise. *So long as the Power lasts.*

Announced today, amidst drizzle and shining walkways: another hundred and fifty highly skilled operatives have been sent off to Three. That makes over a thousand in half a year. It's supposed to be finished soon; if it isn't, we won't be told it hasn't been till afterwards. *Good morning. It was announced today . . .* The retirement age has been lowered by four months. Fears concerning rocket emissions and damage to the upper atmosphere are unjustified. A schoolchild has simplified the standard memory circuit. Between the announcements, I slept, making a point of getting up now and then for something to eat. The old have nothing to do, and there aren't many of us, and we hide.

On Island Paradise in the airport bar, it's the day we would have gone home. The beaches and bars are open, but empty. The holiday-makers prefer the airport, which seems nearer home. The killer hasn't been found. Every confession has been disproved. Accusations have begun to flow, but again, none can be substantiated. We are stuck here, the director of Holiday Flights (Paradise) says pointedly to the chief of Surveillance, until the matter is *competently resolved.*

'We're not accustomed to dealing with emergencies,' he replies stiffly. Emergency. It's getting worse.

The holiday-makers are singing to keep their spirits up. The rumour goes: *It's obvious: she was sick; she killed the woman in the tent and then she killed herself, they found her shoes on the cliff: why can't we go back and try to forget it all?* Why can't we go back anyway? Our lives are at risk, we want to go home –

Kim shouts, 'I know her. She wouldn't. She couldn't have, not herself or anyone else –' (And he's right: when it came to it, I couldn't. But I've lived ever since with someone who could.) 'She said she was happy. It wasn't her. I know.' It must have been, he adds under his breath, 'him': Jo's young man, 'alibi or not', who sits quietly at the edge of the crowd. 'Arrest him!' Kim shouts, but no one takes his orders. I can see the veins on his face swell and throb. This is his moment and I like him for it.

Outside, unseen, there's a kind of lightening in the sky, bluish, brighter, brighter, then gone.

Kim breaks a bottle over the steel counter and rounds on the Surveillance officer beside him.

H and I were walking in the forest. Though sheltered from the glare of the sun, it was residually warm, like a bed just left. Palms shot up through a lower mass of shrubs and broad-leaved trees. Beneath our feet crumbled bark and twigs, here and there a scattering of small orange and brown fruits. We could just hear waves breaking back on the shore, but little sound seemed to come from inside the forest itself. We were walking, hand in hand, unspeaking in this warm dappled silence.

'You think it was me,' Kim says. 'You think it was me, you bastard.'

There's a pause. 'I'm going to kill you,' he says. It's as if the voice isn't quite his own, as if it's speaking from within him.

'Clear the bar' – Surveillance, unnoticed, have moved to stand in a ring about him. The first holiday-makers stumble out into the airfield. They stop suddenly beneath a sky strangely dark. They begin coughing. Thick dust is falling, settling on their skins, dulling the gleam of the planes. There's a distant roaring sound, a feeling of instability, something shaking – they double back, crush with the others emerging. Behind them, inside, the

Surveillance officer shoots Kim; she aimed, she will say later, to disable him, yet she shoots him several times through the neck just as the people outside run back in, coughing from the dust, witnesses one and all. . . . What's happened, what's happened? Inside, as outside, disaster, mystery; oh, take us home, take us away from Island Paradise. . . . Surveillance, in the white uniforms of peace, surround the body – quick – a cloth, a sheet, water – but too late: everyone's seen Wilfully Inflicted Untimely Death a second time, the spattering of blood now drying in the heat. Kim, poor Kim. The bartender, comatose in the bar cabin of the plane (he's come to prefer it there), wakes.

This is how it must have been. Of course, it never would appear on the announcements: *Good evening. It was announced yesterday that a man suffered Wilfully Inflicted and Untimely Death at the hands of a Surveillance officer, and strange dust fell on Island Paradise – where there have now been two Untimely Deaths – there is no explanation – isn't it awful? – what does it mean?* – No, there was no announcement, and still no one could go home. Surveillance rearranged themselves around the sides of the room, as if nothing had happened.

H and I stopped walking. Ever so faintly the earth seemed to shake beneath our feet. We stood, feeling it, looking at each other. About us, the broad waxy leaves of the forest began to rattle in a sudden gust of wind. It seemed darker, then lighter. Cooler, then hot. The air smelled faintly of ash. Still we stood, each reading in the other's face for confirmation of what we felt. There was a great sigh and crash, like a huge wave breaking on the beach, then silence.

Penned in the lounge, the holiday-makers brush dust from their skin, crowd behind the bar to drink and splash themselves with water. The body's gone but they walk round where it was. They talk in whispers, gather in huddles. They are gentle with each other's shock. When they look up, they see the white unsullied uniforms, the careful faces of Surveillance, the strange dusk outside. Accompanied by two officers, the director of Holiday Flights (Paradise) comes in person to make an announcement. She's holding a scrap of paper, and begins to read.

'We are very sorry –' It's as if her apology reactivates the day's events.

'What's happened? We want to know! Please!' a red-faced man erupts, shaking. The murders and the dust have stolen his world. Films of Time Before run in his head. 'We want to go home.'

'We ask you to wait. There is no information. Just wait quietly, please. There will be compensation for –' What's she going to do? She doesn't know what's happened. It's beyond responsibility. But one thing she does know, in her bones and blood, is they mustn't go home, not like this, not –

'There's an IF store to the west, isn't there? It's a research place, isn't it? For dismantling –'

'We demand to go home! It's bad for the children. None of us did it. We're all innocent –'

'Quiet! Quiet please!' The director too is frightened. But she keeps her fingers from shredding the paper she holds. She stands up straight and looks about her at the floor of the lounge patterned with dusty footprints, the bar areas awash with water, the grime-streaked faces of the holiday-makers. She feels their panic, but separates herself from it. It can't go on. Someone must take responsibility, decide, send them home or else –

There's a shriek: 'We're all going to Die Untimely!'

She draws breath, and lies.

'Extraordinary weather conditions are suspected responsible for the dust outside; further information will emerge. Please wait calmly, and stay indoors until further notice. Staff will be sent to clean up, and a light lunch will be served. We regret the inconvenience and distress caused, but there is absolutely no need for alarm.' She smiles, looking from face to face, and nods her head gently. 'Thank you.'

All eyes follow her out of the room, her neatly cut hair, her tailored uniform, dove grey, and afterwards it is quiet.

The bartender watches from the cockpit of the grounded plane, his laughter turning suddenly to tears.

'I don't know,' said H. 'Why d'you think I should know what's happened!' We hurried through the trees back towards the sea.

Emerging, we shielded our eyes against the glare of light. Just beyond the last trees was a line of debris: seaweed, dead fish, waterlogged driftwood, all coated with a thick skin of damp sand. Our few belongings were scattered amongst them. The sea was pinkish brown.

'Some kind of earthquake,' I said. 'Here, your camera. Look, the oars are over here.' H was staring out to sea. *Bird* was drifting carelessly, erratically, away from us.

And on the horizon were two ships, petrol-blue. Without reflection or translucence, they seemed to swallow the light around them. Small launches of the same grim colour dotted the sea about the ships. H pushed me down. 'Get back in the trees,' he said. 'I'm going to get *Bird*.'

'But they'll see you. They might pick you up – wait, let's wait until they're gone –' We strained our eyes; were the ships approaching, receding, stationary? At such a distance it was impossible to tell. But *Bird*, on the other hand, pulled farther and farther away.

'Can't wait,' said H. 'Look, I've got my papers; if they stop me and my pass doesn't cover here, I could make a go of explaining it. But you stay here.'

'But you killed your mother! Don't go. Don't go in the

sea. Why can't we just hide and stay here? H, what's wrong with staying here –?' He pushed me back.

'Go further in,' he said, 'get down.'

It was too late to argue, because one of the launches was heading straight for our once golden strip of sand. I dropped to my hands and knees.

On Island Paradise, the bartender walks across the sun-stricken runway, past the holiday staff, coughing as they sweep and vacuum the dust away, even as more falls, softly now. He enters the smoked-glass bar where the holiday-makers wait, a few slumped disconsolately, the majority agitated and desperately cheerful, moving from bar to window to information office to bar like ducks paddling to save a patch of water from encroaching ice. The drinks are free now, and he helps himself.

'I know how to fly them,' he announces loudly, gesturing at the shimmering planes outside, 'it's all automatic anyway.' The room grows slowly still. Silence falls.

'You want to get out, I'm your person. Who doesn't want to get out? Just say the word.' For a few seconds, his airline uniform commands respect. Their eyes flicker with hope, they swallow expectantly, but no one quite speaks.

'I can tell you, if you don't speak up now, you'll never get home.' One by one they look away. He begins to laugh, perched jauntily on the bar stool, arms and legs neatly folded, grey hair combed back. Surveillance officers standing at the edges of the room stir, exchanging glances.

'OK, OK,' he says, 'joke in bad taste. I'm just as pissed and desperate as the rest of you, but at least I know it. I'll make my way back where I belong.'

'Idiots,' he mutters, quickening his saunter as he approaches the doors, sweating as he emerges into what seemed like magnesium light, total silence.

*

The launch engine cut. I watched three men clamber into a dingy. Four others were visible standing aboard the launch. Binoculars were trained on the beach. H walked to meet the dingy, waving his arms slowly above his head as he did so. The men were armed with small white guns like the one H had thrown away. Their walk up the beach was a slow but determined march. They were all of similar height and stocky build. They sweated profusely, staining their clothes. H shouted to them and waved, but they waited until he stood in front of them before answering.

'That yours?' said the one with the radio, which hissed silence, its aerial whipping tight circles in the breeze. His hand sat steady on his belt. The other two moved to stand either side of H.

'Yes,' he said, his voice pitched higher than usual. 'The anchor must have broken. Why don't you stop her?'

They laughed. 'You're Euro?' His two companions were looking around them. H's tracks led back to the trees. I lay flat on the forest floor. I rubbed earth into my face. 'You shouldn't be here,' he said.

'I've been ill. I went off course.'

'Where's the others?'

'I'm on my own.'

'Come on, you shouldn't be here. You've come out of the holiday zone, well out of it. What are you doing here? Where's the others?' They took a step closer, casting H in shadow. At the base of my spine the muscles twisted tight. I saw his back as he stood in front of them, how small he was in comparison; behind them the launch, the ships, the rest of the world, and *Bird*, bobbing and lurching, smaller and smaller as she inched away.

I felt they could see anything. Perhaps they'd been scanning our escape right from its very beginning: the heat of our bodies, the spectral signature of human flesh, singled out from a tangled mass of data gathered by sensors in the sky, sent high-speed, high-resolution, to the hungry screens below. They can see in the dark. Perhaps they'd seen our faces, our moving lips, our love-making in the night, our almost – quarrels. Perhaps they could see H's gun on the bottom of the sea, a small white shape glowing through green water. Perhaps they could see right through to the end, no escape.

'You shouldn't be here. Where are your cards?'

H steadied hatred and fear against each other, two sheets of brittle glass propped to shelter under in a storm. 'Somewhere over there. It's all been scattered.'

His interrogator walked in front, shirt stuck to his back with sweat, his trousers, slightly faded, straining tight across heavy buttocks. The other two walked either side. Their flesh shook slightly with each step; they were big without being muscular.

'Photographic artist.'

'What the fuck's that?'

'I've done official commissions. I did one for the Force once. You can check. It's all right. I've got a virtually unlimited travel pass,' said H.

'Never heard of a yacht called *Bird*. Been around. Pass covers for almost anywhere.' He passed H's papers to his superior, who said, as he tore them up, 'Not here.'

'Look at the size of him. Wouldn't think he could handle that yacht, would you?' The other two laughed. One of them pushed H; he staggered. No one said sorry.

'You come with us.'

They were smiling. They pushed again, harder; he fell face-down in damp sand. His legs were thin as wire next to their bulky limbs.

'Don't –' he shouted, each of his arms held tight. His feet just skated the ground, kicking the surface of the sand.

'Don't – I've done nothing wrong –'

Nothing wrong, H? Nothing but quietly opened the flap of a tent, looked inside at a sleeping woman with one swollen eye, a powdery face and tiny lines around painted lips, mean, generous, grotesque in the beam of a torch muffled with cloth – and closed it again because he couldn't bear to see. Lay down on damp grass and aimed: the weapon leapt sudden, alive in his hand as it emitted the silent bullet of air that tore neatly through fine fabric. No scream. No exit hole in the other side of the tent. No sign. Just a perforation in cloth, in flesh, that was revenge, rage, erasure, punishment; that was transgression, assertion, separation (that was not enough), that was: wrong? Wrong. I don't know. It probably wasn't like that. You haven't told me. But I don't think it was right.

Island Paradise: *I would like*, whispers the bartender to himself, to sit at the controls and drive that plane smack into the bar lounge. And among the Surveillance officers who stare six hours at a time at the drunken, dishevelled and weeping holiday-makers, their faces sickening with desperation, many find themselves thinking, *I would like to spray them over the wall*, as the hours pass into days. He didn't. They didn't.

'Aren't you ever sorry?' I sometimes say to H.

'No,' he always replies.

It's hard to remember all this. I have the photographs of Jo, I put them in rows on the table. I look at them one by one in the dim glow of the screen and wish she had not been killed, even though it was our beginning.

A Friend

I overslept this morning, and woke feeling hardly alive. I've lumps under my skin, hard as metal they feel. I don't know what they are, and I don't want to. There are other things like that, and worse. I undress as little as possible, in the darkened bathroom. I put cream on my face, neck and arms, as Jo did, but taking more trouble to blend it in. After I'd had some coffee and stared out at the city for a while, it was already late afternoon and I went to stand amongst the crowd watching the day's last announcements. They showed us footage of a speech, made yesterday, or recently at any rate, by Sinco, President of the International Council.

> It is important to remember

he said slowly, leaning forwards, four feet high above our heads. He has jet-black hair, and smooth unlined skin. His face was stern. The rocket and dove gleamed purposefully on his collar.

> not to take for granted the peace and hope and prosperity which we enjoy. It is important, now and then, to remember the past. Only two centuries ago, there were as many as twelve wars simultaneously waged, many people worked spasmodically, not at all, or in unpleasant conditions. Existential disquiet was such that many people lived in misery and uselessness beyond their Times; the population outstripped resources, and, as well as disease,

> Wilfully Inflicted Untimely Death stalked the unkempt streets.
>
> There was so little common ground between nations that vast reserves of energy were squandered in pointless conflict. Now that this is beyond living memory, it is important to recall it consciously. We must beware of nostalgia, for, of course, everything has its price. It is important to value what we have, and to maintain it. It is important for each and every person to understand their situation in relation to the progress we have made and will make, both as debtors, and as providers.

The speech was intercut with the usual old film footage of the dead, and the hungry; hospitals and riots. I felt disorientated: normally history is only for anniversaries, for holidays. Perhaps that's why on this occasion the film shocked me almost as much as it did when I first saw it as a child. *You have to see, you have to know*, they said, *shutting eyes is not allowed.* So that, along with everyone else around me, standing still, limp-faced, I said to myself, no, this must never happen again, and I felt a great surge of guilt at the cynical smile that had played over my lips at the president's opening words. What does my experience matter, I thought, my memories, dreams and voices, my Island Paradise nightmare, my suspicions and sleeplessness and condemnation of Timely Death? What does it matter even if perhaps we are lied to a little bit, if in the dark, in water, near death, we long for proof? Nothing matters if we're saved from *that*. Give thanks. Deliver us. Sorry. Let me pay the Price, all of it, if I have to, I thought; it's nothing. I felt abject, exhausted. There's only one way out of this, I thought. Step over the line. Let go. I could feel what it would be like, lightness in the body, thoughts dwindling to a point, then gone. I shut my eyes.

The crowd began to disperse. I heard someone behind

me clear phlegm from her throat and speak, a mumble really intended for her own ears alone. 'Ha! Be good or else, the man says. That sounds like threats to me.'

I spun round, blinking at the light and colour in the square.

'Hello –' I said eagerly, but her back was turned and already she hurried away. She wore a cap over her hair but I guessed by the set of her shoulders that she was at least as old as me, or as sick. She was weaving deftly between the lingering crowd, which knit gently back behind her. I followed, less agile, more brusque, pushing and apologizing as I went. The dawdling bodies so solid, so inert, that I couldn't get any speed, I couldn't run like I did after H. She was making for the trafficway, easing herself through the group waiting to cross. Beyond the trafficway guardrails, vehicles streamed past, faster than usual, as if to compensate for the lunchtime break, the swish and whirr of their engines sharp in the air. I was close, but all the time more people gathered at the barrier, between me and her. I kept sight of her cap. Her head stood out among the rest. Even now she was tall; once she must have been big-boned, magnificent. A strand of her hair came loose: long, fine, pale-grey at the roots. She shook her head and tucked it back. There was something about the gesture. It's Martina, I thought, pushing forwards, breathless; it is. It can't be. Suddenly the barrier rose and we surged forwards.

'Hey, old woman!' A young man with short blond hair took hold of my arm. 'No need for you to go so fast.'

I shook the restraining hand free. I felt weak. 'Sorry,' I mumbled.

I searched ahead of me, saw her. The tone sounded. She ducked under just as the barrier, two tubular arms, the mesh between them so fine but so strong, descended. Click. It locked behind her. Please wait, the screen said, on off, cadmium light, blinking. Please wait. Traffic resumed. I saw her briefly through the space between two delivery vehicles, smaller already. She had a slight limp. My heart stretched as if there was a bubble growing inside it. I wanted to call out, but I didn't dare. My mouth was dry. By the time the next gap came, she had disappeared. Again the barrier rose, soaring above our heads. Around me, the crowd loosened, flowed fowards; I crossed, although it wasn't where I wanted to go.

At the other side, I rested, exhausted with effort and disappointment. I was sweating hard. The cream on my face and hands had made a brownish rime on my cuffs and collar. It came off on my fingers. Maybe it wasn't her, wasn't Martina, big, callous Martina who wept for the child she couldn't have and steered people like me to their Timely Deaths. Not so likely after all. But it was someone, who said 'sounds like threats to me, be good or else', in a deep whisper, rough at the edges. I played it over in my head, making the voice warm with sympathy, intended, not overheard. I answered with her name. She touched my hand. Come home with me, Laurie, she said, and talk. Sitting on the bench, my mouth was wet, and my lips moved.

'Do you need help?' It was the blond man again. I stared up at him. He was about twenty, grey-eyed. I always notice the colour of eyes. Mottled green, ice-blue, glistening brown like Kim's, mud and gold-specked like Speaker's, muddled hazel like H's, like mine. I wiped the saliva from my lips and chin.

'No, thank you,' I said. He returned my stare, fascinated, horrified.

'No, thank you,' I repeated.

'You shouldn't be out,' he said, swallowing. 'I'm a doctor. You should be at home.' He's followed me, I thought, he thinks I'm dying and should do it at home.

'I'm going home but I don't need any help,' I said, 'but thank you very much.' I knew he'd look back. When he did – I don't know why – but I waved.

I sat a while longer. If not Martina, then at least that was another old person who thinks like me. If I could find someone like that, perhaps I would leave H and live with them. Perhaps others would join us, perhaps –

Of course, now, in the dark, I know that isn't possible. We must live with a younger person to care for us, receive our allowances, and watch them turning into bills if we overstay our Time. I'm lucky, H transfers credit straight to me.

But then, I forgot all that. I leant back on the bench and waited until my legs stopped hurting. I felt grateful to the no threats woman, Martina. I like to think it was her. I lost her to a safety gate, intended to protect me from Accidental Death. That's why I waved at the doctor man, I think. It's crazy.

I stood, uncertain what to do, thinking about the past, imagining it. I thought: was the Unfought War really a mistake? People pushed by me, hurrying home or to drink like H.

Could they have started the Unfought War on purpose? A kind of terrible *threat*, as the old woman put it, given with one hand, and then a sudden rescue given with the other. First the fire to burn, then the water to quench? Even if it was an accident, even if it was, as we're told, a question of accidental launch followed by the threat of escalating counter-attack, then it could perhaps have been an error that was followed by inexorable efficiency. See it this way: the accident, if it was one, was immediately recuperated, it became an example, a huge lesson, and a rescue; tractable, we wept with gratitude to be led away from it, and clutched at the Price, Timely Death, with willing hands. And we've wept ever since. I did it in the square this afternoon, my eyes still hurt.

After all, it's suspicious. For half a century negotiations had required yearly gatherings of leaders moving slowly through a convenient haze of suspicion and recrimination from one definition to another, those strange long words. They made concessions and took advantage, expressed willingness and pessimism, caution and optimism, in an endless calculation towards a balance; but what was in the balance was measured according to theoretical ideas shown annually to be obsolete and superceded. Then the leaders became more friendly. We've all seen the pictures, the huge tables, the majestic platforms, and those leaders kissing each other's cheeks, kissing each other's wives on the hand, shaking hands, raising hands, exchanging gifts and jokes, proverbs and platitudes, smiling – yet still unable to agree from year to year to year. End of an era. The Time of Deadlock, lines growing deeper on their faces.

Yet suddenly, as the long-range weapons hauled themselves into the sky and the defence systems homed in, as the telescreens lost their images and played pre-recorded messages advising us how to hide *in the event* (how everyone screamed, dazzled and blinded: there was finite time and nothing to fill it with but fear), as the nightmare hovered, about to become true, these endless negotiations shrivelled into a short telescreen exchange followed by a month of paperwork. The signing day was marked by weeks of carnival and intoxication. The films we are shown at school and on public holidays, carefully copied and retinted as the celluloid decays, show us those people clinging together in tearful laughter, singing away the shadows of bewilderment, rage and disbelief that fall across their faces. All over the world, and despite the physical and cultural differences so much more marked at the time, people wore that self-same face, astounded and weakly blissful, and we wear the remnants of it now. An orchestrated response to crisis that has become, year by year, a way of life, as if it were written into the fabric of our cells. Suppose. Suppose it wasn't an accident. Suppose I'm right to feel sick when I see film of Time Before, but wrong to feel grateful for now.

Suppose. Island Paradise: the director of Holiday Flights

Inc. stares at the screen image of the secretary of the International Council, recorded and now petrified by the mere touch of her finger on a panel of controls.

'They are very demoralized,' she's just said. 'I'm not sure I can keep the situation stable. There have been Untimely Deaths, violent incidents and strange dust falling. There are rumours of an accident at the IF weapons store and research centre. I have no information. Perhaps it would be irresponsible to send them home like this.'

She is tactful. She doesn't quite know what it is about the world that suggests her particular solution, nor if she's right. She's playing by ear, and it's exciting. He's listened without interruption. Is he giving her permission? Is he asking her to *kill*? His lips hang mid-word. She searches his face, looking for answers in the folds and tucks of flesh, in the way light reflects from his eyes, the faint sheen of perspiration on the larger planes of his skin. What is he asking her to do?

Or does it emerge from inside, that unspeakable image that stirs her blood, turns her steady breathing to a gasp? Is he giving her confirmation? She touches the controls and his face resumes the fluid movement of careful speech.

'Indeed,' he says, 'that would be a *disaster*,' and he looks up, eyes bottom-heavy, staring. Does he incline his head ever so briefly, as if to say *Yes*? She rewinds, freezes again. Even as she touches the controls, observes, considers, and attempts to judge, other thoughts pass through signals, along tracks so polished by use that their progress requires no effort of will. Scarcely aware of what she is doing, she refines her own particular fantasy, elaborates it inexorably to a point where it's become practicable, possible and thence a necessity.

The face on the screen, pronouncing *disaster*, its stare, its nod, offer complicity. It knows something, but doesn't admit it. I can see her face, and it's tighter, more anxious, but trying to be the same. Her breath pushes out sharp between her teeth. *Disaster*: she's always known about disaster, dreamed it, cosseted it. It's invaded her sleep, her daydreams. She's been ashamed, but now such thoughts seem to have a place and a use: perhaps she can do the unspeakable, the illegal, the unheard of, and it will be right. Perhaps it will earn her a place among those who protect the rest of us, who can, perhaps, admit certain things among themselves. She brushes the controls, the dots on the grid gather together and dwindle with a sound faint as falling dust. She summons another image: those grounded planes, cushioned, almost it seems suspended by the heat haze that hovers over the runway on Island Paradise; those planes, dissolving in the heat.

Suppose. Suppose terrible complicit deceptions take place all the time. Suppose they're stacked and layered and spilling out like sheet upon sheet of paper. Suppose this life that goes on about me, this going to work, this learning and play, this world with no killing and no harsh words, this perfectness, this inland city of a thousand screens showing us back pictures of our waiting universe, ourselves going to work, gleaming clean, learning, playing, floating in space – suppose it's all dedicated to something we don't know about, which would make it not there at all, which could make it suddenly worse than a thousand thousand killings. . . . Suppose everyone knows I really needn't pay the Price; suppose on the very day the Treaty was signed people knew that, and nodded and studied faces and kept silence at certain points, testing the wind – I wish I didn't have these thoughts, pushing through me, struggling out day as well as night, I wish I didn't think they were real, I wish we could start the whole thing again, back before I was born, before the Unfought War when we were afraid and could see and name what we were afraid of, before there were paradises that turned out not to be.

It's so hot. H has brought a bottle back with him

tonight and won't go to bed until he's finished it. He's got the headphones on but doesn't seem to be listening. I make him wear them because I've lost my taste for music, but sometimes even knowing he's playing it irritates me. At least he's no enthusiasm for games. The headphones whisper. He stands over me and reads a bit. I turn the page for him but he doesn't continue. I always hope I'll draw him to say something, like 'No, it wasn't like that, he didn't say that' or 'Impossible'. He strokes the back of my neck slowly, beginning light, growing firmer, a rhythm, something to do with the music perhaps. It's soothing. I let my head fall fowards. I can feel sweat run down my face.

After a while I ask, 'Isn't there someone from work you could bring back, once in a while? Can't we risk it?'

Reluctantly, he removes the headphones, filling the air with a thin, soaring sound. The stroking stops, and I repeat the question.

'No.'

'Are you ashamed of me?' I say, but I know it's not that. Anyway, what would we talk about if he did, what could we say to some smooth-faced records clerk saving for a baby?

'I saw someone today that I think I knew once,' I inform him. I want him to know it's possible I could go elsewhere. 'I followed her.'

'Be careful.'

'I would have been all right. She was well over Time.' I watch him as he undresses and climbs into bed; on his skin once perfectly smooth, now a few wiry hairs are breaking out on his shoulders and around his nipples; and perhaps he's a little heavier. Definitely his shoulders stoop: not much, but the beginnings. Sometimes I find myself feeling sorry for him, H, killer. And grateful. I've learned what not to do, that fantasies and dreams of difference, pulling in the mind like magnets, burning under the skin, plucking at the fingers, should be handled carefully, their origins sought. Not only am I all he's got, and I'm old; also, I'm all he wants. I check the locks, straighten the covers, mark his neck with water dipped from my glass. Night. Water.

The launch stayed at anchor, bobbing innocently on the tranquil sea. The name of that blue we had so loved was aquamarine. I lay unmoving and watched, hour after hour. My heart raced, stumbled, stopped; but outside not a ripple changed.

Island Paradise: as the director of Holiday Flights (Paradise) sits alone, eyes closed, preparing the words to use; the would-be passengers have been ordered to remain seated, and to ask permission before urinating. Their meals are brought to them on trays, and the teleset, now mended, is doing a star show. They watch, blank, transfixed, a kind of thoughtless waking sleep. No questions are answered, and they've stopped asking.

Waiting, in sticky heat. Waiting for disaster, for night, for morning, for Time . . . you stumble on a little unevenness somewhere, and find you've torn the fabric of the whole world. You live in a new era of hope, peace, when the natural prohibition against slaughter is for the first time adhered to, and find yourself living with someone who's killed and hearing fights behind every wall. You daren't look at your own skin because it's damp and growing softer, thinner, day by day, but you can't go to the medical centre because they'll want to know how you got it like that. You feel you're living in a lie so enormous and so desirable that nothing can break it: more of a spell than a lie. What to do when you close your eyes and in the midst of a huge and tranquil sea, lapping fitfully, there are petrol-blue ships that shouldn't be there?

⋆

Force personnel stood at ease around the perimeter of the cabin. Its walls were hung with snapshots of other ships, rockets and strange, stubby flight vehicles. Amongst these were several lavish studies of explosions at sea and a single landscape: a mound-shaped island at least half-encased in concrete. There was only one window, through which H could see clouds forming, the first for days. From outside the cabin came sounds of taped music and talk; now and then a splash of laughter. An officer sat at the desk.

'I was blown off course,' H lied.

'Come. There's been no high wind for several weeks. I'm interested, tell me what you saw yesterday. Describe it in your own words, and what it made you think of,' he said.

'I saw nothing. I was unconscious. But on the beach . . . it looks as if there might have been a storm, or an earthquake.'

'You saw nothing.'

'Nothing,' H said carefully, as if placing the word firm and square on his desk. But there were two answers: *I saw nothing* or *I saw something but will say nothing*. For him to accept either required a predisposition in his favour that H had no reason to expect. It began to rain, huge drops streaking the plate glass. H's mouth soured. Outside, it grew darker. A swell was building up, the launch began to roll.

The officer said, 'Beautiful little blast, wasn't it? You must have been terrified, you must have thought your end had come Untimely. I bet you thought that. But it was a long way away, and ever so small. Nothing, really. And no one would've noticed a thing, if the wind hadn't changed, and if you hadn't been where you're not supposed to be. . . . You might as well sit down. Don't you want to know more about it? Wouldn't it be nice to know?'

'No,' said H.

The sea comes high up the beach, takes back some of

its debris. The launch shows no lights. I move deeper into the forest.

Island Paradise: in the fierce grip of her sanctioned nightmare the director of Holiday Flights issues refuelling instructions. The planes, she says, will make an extra stopover, there is no need for total capacity. All the passengers are to go, and all staff but herself. Her voice is light, she makes a couple of jokes.

Two Surveillance officers walk into the middle of the lounge and re-arrest Jo's young man. This time he does not protest, and the man who provided his alibi before looks uneasily in the opposite direction. So what, he thinks, so long as there's an end to this waiting.

The air in the bar lounge hums, the telescreens flicker into life. *The killer has been found*, the director announces. The Surveillance officer shot in self-defence while under stress. Data from meteorological satellites have explained the strange dust that fell. She enjoys the soft, level tone of her voice, a voice she's heard all her life but never used before.

> Holiday-makers should return to the site to collect their belongings. It is deeply regretted that their stay on Island Paradise was disturbed by tragedy and random events. It is understood that their memory of their visit to the Island will be corrupted by what has taken place; a stopover at another luxury resort has been arranged, gratis, in compensation. Tonight we will all sleep well, and tomorrow we will depart.

The gathering in the lounge stirs, as if morning had come. I see them stand up and stretch, turn to their neighbours and smile, vaguely. Already they are forgetting; the sun shines from a cloudless sky on golden sands and emerald forests, the photographs will be developed and the dream come true.

One by one, Surveillance leave their posts, mingling, joking with the crowd they've harboured thoughts of massacring. Some of the children are still sullen and shocked; they cling to their parents' legs, looking up at tired faces that tell them it's all over, everything will be all right. The children grip fiercely, their strength surprising. 'Is there going to be another war,' they ask, 'like there was Time Before?' Of course not, there never will be, what made you ask? And the girl who threw a beer glass at her father, fists clenched, eyes half-closed with weeping, says she wants to stay on the island alone, she hates her father, she hates her home. But, of course, she's told holidays always come to an end, and everyone stands and waits until she's sorry. Little Stella, white-faced and silent, bruises on her arm, watches, trying to understand . . .

'But none of you poor bastards'll ever get home,' the bartender shouts. He makes a fist at the telescreen, now showing the usual images of the earth seen from above. The colours are vivid – reds, blues, purples, edged with orange and green, the colours of heat rather than light. *Space*, a female voice whispers huskily, *the international arena in which even the most daring of humanity's dreams are turned into reality . . . in the absence of gravitational force* . . . He jumps on to a bar stool, raises his arms as if to summon assistance from the planets themselves: 'You're fools to believe her – you think that dust was *weather*? Don't you feel sick and faint? Don't you wonder what's really with the world, with the space outside, secretly, where no human eye can see? What do those bloody colours mean? – Look at your children's eyes, look how terrified they are –'

Surveillance act as if he wasn't there. The lounge empties as he speaks. The planes are waiting to take everyone away. The children are frightened of him as well.

Fire

Last thing yesterday we saw President Sinco and Secretary Vincent making an announcement. They sat at a fiercely polished black table with a small vase of flowers between them, and a huge rocket and dove banner done in blue, white and grey hanging behind. It rippled gently as if they were sitting in a draught.

> There have been allegations, there have been rumours and an atmosphere of suspicion,

they said, looking at each other, then us, taking the phrases turn by turn, as if they were two tones of one voice, and declining to say what the rumours and suspicions were, who made them. I thought it was only me, mad me, and I've never made them to anyone but myself. And H of course. Vincent's red hair blazed, Simco nodded vehemently as he spoke.

> We must dispel this atmosphere. We must live and work in an atmosphere of trust or else we will lose everything we have gained.

That was all. The other old woman wasn't there, but I know what she would have whispered to herself. People looked puzzled, then their faces slackened as a series of prize-winning inventions were displayed. What d'you suppose all that meant? I asked a young man with green eyes standing next to me, forcing him to tear his eyes briefly away in order to see who I was. My voice sounded high, as if I was restraining a cough. 'Live and work in trust,' he said a touch impatiently, 'the importance of unity. What it said. What's the matter? D'you need help?' 'No. Sorry.' The sound hardly emerged. I edged away. Help. Help! I remember saying that to the bartender. I watched the young man looking, the same kind of expression on his face as he might have when looking into a mirror: half absent, but at the same time gently absorbed. On screen, someone drifting out of gravity in a special hyperthermal overall. Then diagrams of a new protein chain. I felt like a stranger, someone from another earth who would never understand. We dispersed quickly, there was a faint drizzle and the evening seemed unusually cold.

It's autumn. New colours, yellows, ochres, orange, fluttering from some of the trees in the square, and people are wearing coats to match. From above the crowd at the crossing where I lost Martina might almost be drifts of leaves gathered by wind, then tossed suddenly across. Formerly, I would have been down there, wrapped in russet, waiting for the barrier to rise. *Establish a perspective. . . . Let go. . . .* I'll order a coat. H already has one, a bit too big, unless that's the style, thickly padded, a muddy cadmium orange, colour of dying embers. It almost smells of smoke. Fire's another way to end. Another dream of destruction; no: the same, in different hues. Tiny, cradled flames in the square, a splash of fuel. Whole cities, roaring. The hungry sun, restless in a dark cave. I know a bit about fire. So does he.

'Yes,' – H has been reading – 'yes, you saved my life,' he says, flat and scornful. So he knows this story really. An admission of sorts. 'You did indeed. Want to take it back? Like we agreed? Isn't it time?' The coat swallows him, his pinched face, tiny hands; it transfixes me.

'Not yet.'

'Why?'

'Because.' The line from the film comes back to me. 'Because, in an emergency –'

'What emergency?' He takes off the coat of fire, nearly throws it on the bed, whoosh, we could all go up – then hangs it obediently on the hook.

'In an emergency, *Trust me*.' The two voices together, the melting eyes, the stars, the rocket rising. Music, call for music! He hasn't seen it, but I'm beginning to laugh, and it's not an entirely pleasant laughter. I grab the coat from its hook, thrust it on. The red scarf too, I wrap that round my head in a turban. Raise my arms, spin round.

'There have been rumours and an atmosphere,' I declare, still spinning, 'A new kind of overall – work together –' I catch H by the shoulder, try to set him spinning as well.

'Stop it – Laurie – stop shouting.' He struggles away. So be it. People do shout. At night. I'm proving it. Hands above head, whirling.

'I'm Vincent –' a rising flame, 'I'm not afraid –' stamping my feet on the floor, spinning, the coat flares about me, the room goes red. I can't stop laughing. I collapse, dizzy, on the bed. He rolls me out of the coat, hangs it up, lies down beside me, looking at me, carefully watching as I catch my breath and the room lurches to standstill. Inwardly I dare him to suggest the usual again, light by the window and so on. I feel angry, and powerful. Our eyes meet and hold. For a few seconds, we are each other. I don't dare speak. This is what it's like, I try to say without words, by thinking at him as hard as I can. At last, he looks away. I unwind the turban myself. My head feels lighter.

I got some relief; H looks restless, hasn't spoken since. But I am almost peaceful, and I'll go on with what happened. I'm breaking a treaty, but it wasn't much of one. We agreed to forget, but I haven't. Neither has he; he just pretends, sneers, and often, now, he watches over my shoulder.

*

Night. I was waiting, alone on our island. For morning, H's return, wreathed in smiles, escaped again; or an empty sea, ships gone, left behind. The soft throb of an engine reached me, coming or going, I wasn't at first sure; then laughter, shaken hollow by its journey over water. I heard the scraping of a dingy pulled up the beach. I thought they'd come for me. If H was with them, why so quiet? Had they come for me? Had he betrayed me? Or perhaps, even, it was all alright. I grasped handfuls of earth and squeezed them to dry pellets in my palms, water running out between my fingers. Twigs snapped. Two of them, close.

One said, 'Shit. What's wrong with here? No need to go too far in, can't see my own feet.'

A wave of fumes spread through the air, heavy, sickening.

'Sort of thing you dream about, isn't it, but it's not the same on orders. Quick.'

Slowly, I stood, peering into the blackness. Then, as they were blundering, panicking their way back through the forest, a line of vivid flame shot up, roaring and gasping for its air. I rushed forwards, falling, tearing my skin. An engine coughed into life. The damp vegetation hissed and sputtered. H was a small black bundle, growing fainter in the orange glare. They had wrapped him in a blanket, the flames were beginning to bite. The fire swirled and rolled, an orgy of smoke and steam. He was unconscious or dead. The hairs on my face and arms shrivelled. My hands slipped from him as I dragged him away. I could see our flesh smarted and swelled like something boiled, but I felt nothing. I beat the fire from his feet. We were sweating petrol, gritty, astringent, our breath drew the flames, they followed us step for step. *Sorry*, I kept saying, *sorry*, as I twisted his limp body, crushed it accidentally into trees, fell on him; *sorry – help me, you're not –*

When my legs were incapable, nothing but weight, I turned and saw the fire far behind us, its flames pointing away: the wind was on our side. I saw it through a grid of tree trunks that looked like bars erected to keep it back. I lowered H to the ground, straightened his limbs. I felt the wind on my back, the coolness of evaporation. His pulse eluded me, absent or drowned by my own. I breathed into him, again and again. Something panicked beneath the tight skin of his chest, clutching at a rhythm. Parts of my body, separated by their different tasks and tirednesses, slowed down, came together again. I lay close to pass on my warmth.

Yes, I saved it, and I won't take it back.

Last night the red scarf was lying tangled over the bed where he slept. What's it worth, his life? I thought. What's the real price? Pretty low, I thought.

Before it was properly light this morning, the public telescreen began to wail, summoning us to emergency announcements; though we didn't know it was emergency as we skeltered down the stairs, it might have been a holiday, a discovery, more miracles of science. The last time it happened I was still at school, and they had invented gossamer transmission cable. You run because the noise is so awful and you think that if you get there quickly it'll stop. From our Residential I saw people I never knew were there, some rushing out scarcely dressed, holding toothbrushes and cups they'd been using when the sound began. We ran to the screen all together, other groups emerging from nearby Residentials. We looked at each other, our faces transformed by the abnormal. The huge screen, blinking in time to its scream – I wanted to shake it into life, but we had to wait, aimless, noticing our disarray.

At last. Since yesterday, Sinco and Vincent have gone. A new secretary and a new president, the result of two sudden but Timely deaths. But we all knew it couldn't be that: new appointments occur regularly, even important ones, and wait for the scheduled announcements.

The new faces briefly flashed, not smiling. A deep breath from the announcer. He spoke flatly. New facts, discovered only yesterday: there is someone, or something, else after the resources of Planet Three! The crowd, stunned silent, jostled and stretched to see – but there are no pictures of it. This entity is aggressive. Our new president appears still unsmiling. I've forgotten his name. He's younger than any I remember, golden-brown skin and bright, aniline blue eyes that fix us one and all. We will see something that will shock us, he warns, but ignorance is not bliss: we live in a real universe, a terrifying hugeness of space, and must know its dangers in order to match ourselves against them.

Some stills, grainy, black and white: an extraction platform on Three. The same platform, torn to bits, melted, and, floating above, attached by cables, the lifeless bodies of technical workers, their arms and legs splayed in a child's dream of flight, their silvery suits disfigured with black and brown stains. I tried to count them. My heart beat faster.

On screen, the new president turns to us gravely, as if he's been watching as well. We must not panic. Precautions are being taken. We must not panic, but our survival may be at issue. The situation tends towards one of conflict. Power must be stringently conserved, commencing with the domestic supply. Areas to be switched off on a rota basis. No cause for panic. He is confident, he says.

The crowd turned to look at itself; most faces were alert and strained, as if after a happy but sleepless night. An emergency. We said the unfamiliar word to ourselves and each other, feeling the thrust of our lips: it had to be pushed out. Our cheeks glowed in the morning chill. Fingers through hair, tidying, feeling, reluctant to go back home.

Doesn't seem real.

What'll we do in the dark?

It's like our blood supply.

Something Else out there, something else.

When we turned to look out it was surprising to see, like a sudden appearance of spring flowers, the white uniforms of hundreds of Surveillance against the black of marble, the rich gold of dusty glass caught by the morning sun. In twos and threes people dispersed, folding their arms across their chests, pulling their inadequate clothing tight against the breeze. Their faces all question and wonder, no panic. Why's that? I thought. The answer, probably, is that those clear blue eyes inspire confidence. He said there is no cause for alarm.

It's like being in the films of Time Before. The immediacy, the shock. Overwhelming in itself, the sheer volume of information. I wish it was written down, I can't remember the exact words used; when it's about nothing, I can. There's something else in the universe, wanting our Power. Two members of the Council changed overnight. The thing, whatever it is or looks like, *kills*. The Power may run out. Nothing working. No Progress. Overnight we live in a different universe, and surely life on Planet One, the earth, will have to change to match it? It can't be grasped, but my heart beats faster, and I think I like it. Can't keep still. All day I kept looking out, going for short walks to the square and back. This is as important as the Unfought War.

What will they do, our new president with his blue eyes, our new secretary with glasses, with a thing on Three that kills?

This evening, H returned drunker than usual. I shook and shook him, trying to stop him going to sleep. He was dribbling, his tightly boned face was rimed with a day's sweat.

'It's all happening. Did you see?' I kept saying.

'I know, I know.'

I gave in. I felt I didn't need him to talk so much as I

usually do. It grew dark. Our block is off, proving what was said. There's something gone in H, like he's off as well; truth is it's been like it for years but it hasn't mattered so much till now. It was part of the world but now the world is different, there's something else on Three. I cried a bit. I walked round the room feeling the walls in the dark. I raised the blind: nothing.

What will happen?

What will they do?

How can they explain what they do, if they do what I think they might? Will the it or they come here?

My heart beats like an engine, faster, faster. I must check the locks, straighten up. For almost a whole day, there has been something else on Three, wanting our Power. I'm writing in the dark, by hand. It makes a faint sound; tonight there is no other.

Storm's Eye

Production figures. Science in Schools festival, overalled children with their hair tied back pottering officiously in labs, clipboards, monitors, screen on screen on screen. I want to smash them: day after day, nothing.

'Come off it,' says H when I shake him awake in the middle of the night. 'How d'you know it was even true?'

'I don't care if it is or not. You look awful. You stink. Why d'you always get drunk?' As if I didn't know. I feel malicious.

'I get pissed because I feel like shit and I don't really care. Let's do it now, you know . . .'

'Shut up. There wasn't any Power last night. When you look back, there was always something wrong with Three, delay after delay.'

He goes to work in the morning, comes back the same. Left to himself, he'd die Timely all right. Power's on, it's off. I search the streets for the other old woman; fruitless. I imagine she's Martina. I could talk to her, I could *check*. I could hold her tight. We could push open a window, wrap our heads in red scarves, and scream. But she's not there. In fact, there seem to be less people about, a great lull, a hush. At night too, it's quiet. No muffled screams, no low rumble or argument, just the November wind blowing hard, as if we were whirling disconnected in space . . . as if we were hiding. As if we were in a deeper peace than ever before, a thick, gluey liquid flowing in fast and rising above our heads.

How can they tell us that and then no more? Did I dream that there is something else on Three? Did I just make it up as I sat here in the dark, with nothing happening, wanting it to? Did I dream that word, emergency? There's no record, I can't check. Do other people just forget things, day on day? I should ask someone, some stranger. Do you remember, a while ago, they said on the announcements? – but I'm scared to look into one of those passing faces, so smooth, like mine was. 'What?' they might say, arching their eyebrows, counting the lines, noting the strange blotches on my face. They're all young.

And I got a card from Age Counselling, the first. I won't go, I can't go, I don't know what's happening. As ever, there's always the past, bright and clear, and not even mine. I sit here and see things, some of which I wasn't there to see. H is no use, won't confirm or deny.

'It's all the same to me,' he lies, turning away.

Island Paradise, Island Paradise, emerald green: I see Jo's young man sitting alone, locked in one of Surveillance's offices. He puts his glasses on, takes them off, cleans them. The first time they arrested him, he had been standing at the edge of the sea and he'd noticed *Bird* had gone. Jo might have gone too, he thought, and he wanted to find out. He never meant to lose her. He enjoyed their relationship, particularly the fights. Four of them had come to get him and because he'd all but done it, dreamed it often enough, he couldn't believe it when they let him go. When he was released, his alibi had walked across the lounge and taken his arm, but he'd pulled it angrily away and refused to speak to him. On his alibi's face he glimpsed the same look of shocked pleading that Jo used to wear.

Now they've arrested him again, but no one's come to see him or ask him questions. Time passes. He scarcely remembers Jo, who brought him to Island Paradise, just her bruised face, the way she pronounced certain words. She escaped him, he lost her to someone else: H. He is beginning to ask himself whence comes his fantasy of killing by little inches of cruelty. He is beginning to guess what happened, and what will, but no one will ask him now. His skin is brown from island sun. The pride has slipped from his face, leaving it slack and soft-looking like a child's.

Recently, I asked H what he knew of him.

'Nothing,' he said, always his opening move, then grudgingly added, 'Jo met him in her lunchbreak, at the Tech theme park. They watched the announcements together. They played on with lasers, they met later and went to bed. She always wanted him to live with her, he never would. I told him to leave her alone. He said no one but her could tell him that and she never would. He was right, as it turned out.'

'I met him on the beach,' I said. 'My tent was near theirs. I heard them arguing. I hated him.'

'He was just ordinary. It was her I hated,' H said. It's silly, but it hurts me when he says that.

Island Paradise, sparkling in turquoise sea. The day of departure. Very early, the holiday-makers and island staff form into orderly queues. I see them holding their tickets and mementoes – a video portrait of Paradise, pictures of trees, glass tubes filled with coloured sand. They feel the hours together in the lounge have brought them closer, and now everyone shares relief and excitement. They wonder where it is they are going, the Golden Desert, the Mountain Tops, the Purple Plains? The killer will be *erased*, adults explain, just the same as the function on a keyboard, so that the same thing could never happen again. Another little contradiction everyone ignores. The larger of the planes slowly taxies nearer. The director of Holiday Flights comes down to bid them goodbye as they cross the stretch of sweltering tarmac between the coolness of the lounge and the air-conditioned aeroplane. She shakes their hands: 'Enjoy your flight.'

'Thank you. We'd love to come back to Island Paradise another year.' They screw their eyes against the sun, hurry up the ramp.

'I wonder what's happening at home . . .'

'Nothing, I should think. A lot of fuss about the southern Council elections. Launch of that power satellite. Anyway, there's another week before we have to go back.'

'Did they have that dust at home too?'

'I shouldn't think so, darling.'

The stewards begin the safety demonstration: 'Air travel is the safest transportation method there is. However, in the unlikely event of engine failure, a tone like this will sound . . .' No one listens.

'They ought to make the weather the same. They could make it sunny all the time. Where do they go?'

'Who?'

'The people who are ki –'

'Into the air of course, like anyone else.'

'Is the weather made of people, then?'

'Stella, sit still –'

The bartender, setting out goblets ready for the rush, finds his hands gripping them too hard, he can't let go, the brittle plastic cracks. In the pilot's rest-room, Jo's young man, sitting on the vacuum pack that contains her body and flanked by two Surveillance officers, tries to catch their avoiding eyes. 'I bow down my head,' he shouts. 'I want to confess –'

The engines whine, throb, scream, drowning his words. The aeroplane turns slowly, tilts the aerofoils on its wings, then pelts, lights flashing, up the runway. Through the windows, the airport buildings, markers and the trees that surround them blur and streak, as if Island Paradise were being wiped away. They're up, slicing through empty sky. The hard line of white exhaust behind them softens and expands. The director of Holiday Flights waves, then hurries to the flight controls, where the plane full of people is a moving pinprick of blinking light crawling across steady concentric lines.

So, there's something else after the riches of Planet Three, but everything's normal. It was then, too. *Back home*, the friends and relatives of the people in the aeroplane, their return delayed by technical difficulties (*lucky bastards*), worked and played as hopefully as ever. Children went to school and learned mathematics, oceanography, food technology, post-war history, keyboards, structures, physics, administration, biotech, realist ethics. A busy world, reaching out, further away; adults who had already learned these things put them daily into practice. As I once did, as Jo once did, they worked mainly in light tech, supervising equipment, refining processes of manufacture, or in design, data collection, agripractice or research. There were the usual local differences, based on the availability of resources, in the way people spent their working lives, variations in the texture and quality of life. The cities, though massive, were clean and built to give an illusion of space. Doctors treated people for minor ailments: tics at the corner of the mouth or eyes, sudden lapses of short-term memory. The Council of southern nations was being re-elected following the deaths of two members. The northern Council was in session, arguing lengthily over the distribution of certain orbits between the member states. The birth rate was down, the crime rate still negligible but slightly up. The most popular entertainment that year was synchronized laserplay.

To think I, Laurie Hunter, played with lasers too, and enjoyed swimming with Kim or Martina two or three times a week. To think I once stood casually in front of the public telescreen eating a lunch bar and forgetting within minutes what I'd heard and seen. I remember there were smaller screens then, and the resolution not so good. To think that then, when I closed my eyes to sleep, all that swirled before them in the few moments before sleep was a faint print of the circuits I'd been examining that day, intriguingly superimposed, a record of placid concentration on the task in hand. To think I never wanted anything different, when now all I do is hope for change, at any price. To think that now I, once dreamless, sometimes toss and turn and mumble so much I wake H, as a light or a dropped glass will not. In the dead of night he wakes and comforts me, not angrily at all.

'Sorry,' I say, befuddled into using a word I now avoid.

'You can't help it. I used to have bad dreams,' he whispers, 'after that night –' *It happened.*

Thin ghosts of smoke hung in the air, but the fire was out. I saw the damage I had tried to see with my fingers in the night: a rib's end nudged beneath skin that was bruise-blackened like a rotten fruit, one arm broken in several places, his face unrecognizable. The soles of his feet were burned. He opened his eyes, bloodshot and set in darkening flesh. I touched him; sweat broke out over his entire body; I felt the surge of nausea that's my own response to physical pain.

I found water, tried to clean him and tie a splint on his arm. His body was limp; a jumble of words and half words, one angry, the next pitiful, fought their way through his swollen lips. There was no sense in it. His face clenched tight with each effort to speak, becoming a mass of sore flesh carved by straining lines.

'Ssh,' I said. I thought he was dying. I wasn't sure he knew who I was. We were reduced to nothing.

'They let it off on purpose. Told me – we're just waiting – never been stopped –' he managed to say, before he was lost again.

On purpose. Wilfully. As with his other announcement, *I killed someone this morning*, I easily accepted what I would have declared to be impossible before my holiday flight. You've bought me much bad news, H, though it's not that which makes me angry with you. When I despise you, want to push you away, when I think I should walk out of the door and never come back, after all, we're just hanging on, it's not because of that. It's because you don't do it any more. Because, when they said 'Wouldn't you like to know?' you replied 'No' so as not to give them the satisfaction. But I'd like to know. And they got their satisfaction anyway; they beat you flat and left you for dead and the officer turned a blind eye; miles away from anywhere, yachts often sink.

H was staring at me.

'Someone's watching,' he whispered. I glanced behind me just in case.

Six or seven people, all dressed in tarnished metal-grey overalls or the remains of them. Some had no more than a few scraps left, tied with string to cover the feet, shoulders and chest. A woman stepped silently out of the shadows into a patch of light. Her face, framed with blue-grey hair, belied the youth of an upright and strongly muscled body.

'Your friend alive? Your boat's sunk. You can't stay here.' The others drew nearer as she spoke. I noticed that some were armed, but they approached very slowly, with their hands folded across their chests.

'This island's not safe. It's burning. Come with us,' she said, handing me a small package, which contained an overall like theirs.

'The fire's out. I think he's dying . . .' I said, beginning to cry.

'Put it on. The fire's never out,' she replied. 'No one lives here. Come.'

A tall thin man with a limp that made him sway eased H on to a stretcher while I supported his half-bound arm. He fought feebly against us, screaming in a whisper and trying to avoid our hands. Without a word someone pushed me forward and the group became a column, a thread weaving its way through the trees. I knew it was the last I would see of our island: at first it seemed poignantly beautiful, but our rescuers, their shoulders hunched, their heads down, they had no time for the clusters of red and purple flowers, the softness of filtered and refracted light. They walked as if we were in a long dark tunnel, a distant patch of light ahead, a tide of stinking liquid rising about our feet. Their urgency was contagious. *The fire's never out* . . . I couldn't bear to fill my lungs with the place's air; I breathed scantily, the blood began to pound in my head. My flesh crept when dew-spattered leaves brushed across my face. In some places, the smell of the fire still hung trapped in the dense layers of vegetation, and in the invisible suspension of water in the air. Ahead of me, H began calling, sometimes to Jo, sometimes to me, his voice harsh and relentlessly regular, then falling suddenly silent, only to recommence its chant.

I see the pilot glance at his watch. He loves flying, despite the increased automation. He loves to press in a code, ease a dial home and feel the plane turn, sink, accelerate, to see the information dials winking the expected figures. It's so perfect, like making a symphony every day all on his own.

'We are changing course now, heading north for the Golden Desert Holiday World,' he declares. The controls move. The dials do not, they hold as if glued, set on the course for home.

In the crowded bar lounge, the bartender, sober and silent, measures drinks without pause for breath or thought, and everyone swallows a toast to the Golden Desert, those empty and majestic plains, those scalding days and stardust nights, those sculptures made by wind and time in sand and rock.

*

'The water was such a very clear blue, wasn't it?'

'We felt so free lying next to it, away from everything ordinary.'

Three people died Untimely, but one was suicide and one was self-defence, and the man that started it will be erased; soon the waves will wash it all away.

No special entertainments this time, just the usual in between announcements stuff, ethereal music, planets swirling in space. I think the planets are so much bigger than the pictures of them on a telescreen. The planets are faraway and foolish things to pin dreams upon. There is something else on Three. Wilful.

'There's no response,' the pilot says to the director, now acting flight control, the threads of all their dreams in her hands. He turns knobs full circle, pushes switches to their extremity as he speaks.

'Check your systems,' she says.

The pilot tries to establish contact with mainland controllers, but can't get through. Nothing is operational except the fuel gauge, slowly sinking. The music of flight is becoming the backwards babble of rewound tape, faster, faster.

'Island Paradise, Island Paradise, are you overriding me, are you jamming me?'

The director doesn't answer, though her heartbeat's as wild as his, her skin as damp. She sits alone in the control room, insulated from the heat, from the steady beat of waves on the empty sands, the settling dust. Seen through glare-resistant glass the island is like a film of itself, immaculate. The blinking light progresses painfully slowly across the grid of lines that represents the sea. Warnings flash, are resolutely ignored. *Hurry, hurry.* She can't move, almost can't bear it coming true.

We had crossed the island. The bay we stood in was less

than a hundred yards across. They placed H carefully down in a sliver of shade, then set straight to launching a collection of small canoes and one wider craft with a sail.

So far, no one but the broad-shouldered woman, now crouched, now stretched at the end of her oar, had spoken, and that only the once. The silence suited me. I looked back as we slipped away under the combined power of oars and a woven sail. A faint dirtiness in the air above the island was the only sign of what had happened. On the other side of the boat a small, tired-looking woman rowed. At the far end from where I sat, other oars lay unusued. I offered to take one.

'No,' the woman said, 'give him a drink.'

H's throat moved as I drizzled the water between his teeth, but he seemed worse, his eyes lost in the purple swelling that filled their sockets.

'Never mind,' the woman rowing said as her oar travelled through the air ready for another pull. The tattered overalls were basted to her skin with sweat, 'Not long.' The woman on the other side did not speak, breathing out hard between clenched teeth. I looked about me and across to the other craft. There were more women than men. Some light- and some dark-skinned. In height and shape they were more different from each other than any group of people I have ever seen: tall, short, broad, slight, some amputees or with oddly formed limbs, as motley as the uniform they wore. They were like, I realized with a shock, those people on the films of Time Before.

'Please return to your seats. Please return immediately. Stewards take up position.' The pilot's voice is sharp: very little fuel remains. 'Please remain calm.'

'Why the hell?' says the bartender to himself.

'I have not been able to alter course. We are almost out of fuel. Please put your life-jackets on, do not inflate them yet. Note the position of your emergency exits.'

The passengers are calm, their fingers busy, their eyes wide. They wait. The plane ploughs on through the sky, devouring its last drops of fuel, which seem to last for ever. *Perhaps*, the pilot thinks, *the fuel gauge is faulty. Perhaps we're safe . . .*

In the silence and waiting, a wave of terror sweeps through the ranked passenger seats, pushing their heads into their hands . . .

We are going to plunge into the sea.

We will never arrive.

Never reach the Golden Desert.

Never know . . .

Someone shouts, 'Let me out of here,' and another, 'Get out of the way.'

Please remain seated. Nothing will be achieved –

They stand up, struggle out of the seating into the aisles; they wouldn't obey, they can't bear it. They fight against Untimely Death and its tidal wave of unspent dreams, they beat their fists on the doors, the windows, the stewards, each other; they tangle in the hanging oxygen masks, fall in trampled heaps on the floor. Life-jackets tear, deflate. Faces twist in a frenzy of denial. They pull each other away like veils, trying to see underneath, underneath and afterwards. The bartender, his jacket half-tied, watches. The wail of children's voices rises above the grunts and screams of their parents. Beneath all the noise, the vibration of the engines ceases, unnoticed. The doors slide open. The air outside smells of the sea. The passengers rush and stumble into the sky. The bartender waits, fastening tabs and pulling the string of his life-jacket; all the same, he considers staying.

The pilot shouts, 'Please remain calm.' His voice twists into a scream. 'There's nothing I could do. The controls are being jammed!' Seconds before impact, the bartender steps out, falling free in a rush of air.

Air and water, heavy and light, unmixable, the boundary

absolute, a seamless join, the surface of the water seems to hang like a shining skin they could never pierce, it seems they will just fall and fall – the next second it's torn to shreds that curl themselves in separate bits, slices and chunks of water that spin to sheets and droplets, atoms and molecules, hollow bubbles flying through the air. The sea is gouged and scattered, the air invaded, that perfect edge all gone.

I wonder if planning is what makes a Timely Death. Someone else's planning. I wonder, what happens on the edge of Timely Death? What is it that floods like caustic through the veins? A lifetime's unheeded suspicions and unspent dreams? Is it that which kills the Timely Dead, regular as a plotted curve, that gradual loosening of the grip, that final opening of the fingers, the slack and upturned palm.

H is looking over my shoulder again.

'You'll find out soon enough,' he says flatly. 'What're you doing about this card?' Age Counselling. I didn't tell him. He holds it between finger and thumb. I think he's afraid as we approach the shameful end.

H, you shot that bullet of air, you took me away, you didn't care if we were caught, you were beaten and burned. No, you don't want to look at the pictures you took of Jo, which to me, ache with longing. Once you held a lens to your eye, and I ran through hot sand to speak with you, but now you don't want to see at all. I'm sick of being stuck with you, I'm sick of my world, which is you. I've protected it too long. I want you to go under, weep, explode, leave me free. Before things got so far, and events took over, we should have got it clearer. We should have argued on the beach on our island.

If, one of those silver mornings when I woke first and watched you lying loose, your body shapeless with sleep, and one hand burrowed into the sand as if searching for another to hold, if I'd said as you woke, sitting up to look around you, running your hands through your lengthening hair: 'You're not what you seem. Who are you really? What is it you're for? What do you really want? Where do you come from?'

Then – then, he'd've shrugged his shoulders.

'Don't do that,' I'd've said. 'Answer me. What will happen to me?'

'I've noticed,' he'd've answered, his words even as print, maddeningly precise even as he expresses the inexact and the unknown, even as he avoids me, 'that people ask questions when they're afraid. And address the person next to them as if they were the whole of the world and the whole of time.'

'Where can we go, what've we got left?' I interrupt.

'I don't know,' he says. 'Anywhere.'

'Why should I trust you? You're a killer.' He shrugs.

'Why did you bring me here?' He answers, 'Because you so wanted to come.' That's not quite true, though I know I did. That's what makes me want to break him apart, make him disappear.

'Why did you kill Jo?' I'd say. H stiffens, his shoulders go back, he loses in a moment all the last traces of sleep.

'I hated her,' he states.

'You're lying,' I shout. 'I just want to know. I hate you.'

'You're crying,' he says.

'Tell me something,' I shout, 'tell me anything, so that I can believe you –' My throat burns, I can't keep still, the whole of me fumbles awkwardly for some enormous and violent gesture that would take me elsewhere.

I struggle clumsily to pull the dingy from the oar it's propped on. I can hardly see for tears, the sand and sky run into one single burn of light. I run down the beach, pulling the dingy behind me; H, of course, doesn't try to stop me. I blunder into the water, launch myself towards *Bird*. I'm on board with the dingy pulled up behind me before I turn to look.

He's standing in the shallows, the camera to his eye. I tear up the tarpaulin and shake it overboard, great rumpling slaps of wet oilcloth, I shake and shake. H turns and wades back, past our sleeping place, on and on. He hasn't pressed the shutter. Suddenly he looks like the man I ran after, at the beginning, before I knew, and I want him even though I can only follow him with my eyes until he disappears.

I don't think there's any way out of the way things were or are. I can't dismiss him. I can't go. I know what he is, what he's for. He's heavy, he's silent, he's killed. He's mine. I must keep him safe in this our darkened room, check systems, lock the doors and windows one by one, mark him with water, before at last I sleep. I have no agreements with anyone, I'm doing this on my own.

We rowed into a cave in an island of rock. Several fires were burning, the smoke lost in blackness far above. The sea broke on a gentle slope of glistening black stone, and echoed, faint but continuous, far above our heads.

Other people in overalls were already there. Our arrival was noted but no one greeted us. H was carried to a far corner of the cave. I followed. There was a row of chests, bearing the rocket and the dove, marked through with a careful 'X'. Cancelled out. Dressings, bandages, drugs, were taken out. Pushing me aside, they began to wash him.

I sat alone. Some people sat like me, doing nothing. Some were gutting fish near the mouth of the cave. Others attended to the boats, scrubbing them inside and out, patching small leaks. No one talked to me, or seemed even to notice me. I looked around. Everything was very neat, set out on the floor in rows and lines, evenly spaced. There was a long row of silver packages that I thought might contain some kind of food, and another of inverted bowls. Tarpaulins covered several stacks of boxes or chests, and even the stones used to weight their edges were placed exactly equidistant from each other. This neatness went beyond the functional, though it would have been immediately apparent if anything was missing. And although the effect was somehow decorative, it seemed more than that as well. It was as if objects were displayed with extra space around them so as to say, this is exactly what there is, and how much of it there is. Nothing is hidden. There were oars, stacked and arranged in rows of six, and all around the walls of the cave were painted in white the outlines of human figures, their legs slightly apart, their arms held away from their sides, their fingers just short of touch. Eventually the woman who had spoken to us in the forest approached, and set down two bowls of baked fish. She smiled, and then began to eat, gesturing at me to do the same.

'What are they?' I asked, pointing at the figures. She rose to her feet, and stood in front of one of them. It fitted perfectly.

'Us,' she said. Looking closer, I could see differences in them, though at first they had seemed like the other rows and lines, identical. There seemed many more of the outlines than there were people in the cave.

'Who are you?' I said, after a few more minutes' silence.

'We are the floating people, exiles and escapees. I am Speaker. I can tell you our story, and hear yours, but it will take some time.'

'Yes.'

She smiled. 'That's good.' She paused, cleaning her hands with a scrap of cloth and then said, 'Eat.' She waited until I obeyed before continuing.

'We began some years after what you call the Unfought War. Most of the archipelago was cleared for IF use. Excuse me, I find it difficult to know where to begin. The whole area is variously contaminated, some, but not all of it from what's called Time Before.' She became more confident, as if she'd heard or said these words before. 'But here, there is no Time Before. Time Before is still here, measuring itself in our bodies, shaping our movements, speaking itself through our lips.' She stood up.

'Listen,' she said, raising her arms slightly, like the pictures on the wall. 'Time Before is many voices speaking.' Suddenly we were not alone. Floating people appeared and sat about me and Speaker, each one calm and separate in their own pool of space, just like the oars and bowls about the edges of the cave. Speaker's brow furrowed. She planted her feet further apart, leaned forwards, resting her hands on her thighs. My skin tightened and pricked as she looked at us one by one, as if counting us. She seemed to have grown younger, and heavier. When she spoke again, her voice was deep, almost a growl.

'This is the truth, but no one knows. I'm telling you. I come from a small island, but you won't have heard its name. We lived on our island since the birth of time and they gave us one month to leave. They needed to test something so as to put an end to all wars, they said, and so we agreed. And the wind was blowing the wrong way, which they said was an accident, and they moved us away for a few years, living in metal huts like ovens. But we said it wasn't an accident, we said they wanted to see what would happen. And when they took us back, they said, "Now your island is clean and safe," but it didn't look the same, nothing grew and none of *them* would stay. And we have been sick ever since. They said: "OK, OK, we won't do our tests above ground, we won't use your sacred sites," but they broke their word, and then bought us overnight with millions of dollars under the table, and now we speak their language, I speak it now.

'Our sea is killing us. And we women give birth to babies born like jellyfish. No eyes, heads or arms. In no way human. Sometimes a few hairs on them. And they breathe, they live for a few hours, they die, and we hide them from the mother but she knows. She knows.'

Speaker stood up straight, but she wasn't Speaker any more.

'*This is the truth but no one knows,*' she said, her foot tapping to the rhythm of the words.

'This is the real thing in there but it sounds like a story, we sound mad with our suspicions and our jellyfish babies, yes, it sounds like we're savages dreaming dreams because you all, you're used to believing other big stories you've been told. Why does no one know? Why does no one know?

'Don't cry. Don't cry. That's not what I come for, tears; that's not what I've come to get.

'I've come to get you to knock on the doors of your governments and ask, why did you do that, why did you keep it quiet? You ashamed or what? Why did you lie? I want that you keep knocking on those doors. You plant your feet thick on the ground and you don't move, you won't go away, you say, why d'you tell us lies? Don't tell them any more. That's what I want, that's what you've got to do. Thank you, thank you.'

All about me, the floating people began to clap their hands. But this was not the muddled thunder of applause, it was a slow steady beat in unison. I joined in. Thud, thud, falling between and across the sigh of the waves. Speaker sat down. She gestured at me. I understood that I had to tell my story. I stood, wondering where to begin. I felt I had to translate it somehow, and I felt I didn't know enough. All about me they clapped, steady. I shut my eyes and saw the burning square on film of Time Before. I saw the woman pour fuel over her head and light a match. I raised my arms. A voice came from my lips, thin and bitter.

'I am not satisfied,' I said. 'I am not satisfied. I feel the tissue of lies, the soft and the hard, folding around me, smothering, smothering. I want to wield my screams like killing knives; I dream of destroying, I walk to the centre of power with a bomb between my legs, I die in an ecstasy of exposure, an orgy of transgression, believing it will be different, that's the only moment that's mine. Who am I? I am not satisfied.

'I am living at the end of the twentieth century and I read newspapers still, the ink comes off on my hands, but I can put them down to think and consider. I read that Briggs and Karancheck, Minito and Ellulah agree peace is the only viable condition and that they are determined to attain it ... my heart panics ... I look at their photographs. I do not believe them. There is something standing behind them.

'I don't believe the water is safe, but must sometimes drink.

'I do not believe you have forgiven me or ever will.

'I don't believe in violence but sometimes nurse longings to kill. My hands twitch. They say I'm free to differ. But if I turn their words off, seek my own, seek silence, I'm choking in a vacuum –

'I'm one of many not satisfied. We scream; we scream, for it seems the words don't matter; the volume, the tone, is all that expresses us, the strain and crack. I – just – want – to – know –'

The hard, bitter voice of not satisfied ricocheted about the walls of the cave, blistering in our ears. I dropped to the ground. Not satisfied, the dark side of that smiling woman in a garden of doves – how did I come to be her, to know her? I felt light-headed, listening to the last echoes of that voice that wasn't mine. Speaker looked up at me. We were alone again, sitting opposite each other on the glistening rock. I couldn't be sure it had happened.

'Time Before is many voices. Thank you,' she said quietly.

'After the Treaty, these islands were finally cleared. The Force said everyone must go. No one knows what happened to those that obeyed. Those that refused to go were told that they had no official status, except that they had been warned. They were required to sign a declaration. For a while, scientists wearing suits like these visited; they wanted to study the strange births, new diseases, to see how long we lived. One year, soldiers came instead . . . the remaining people fled; that was our beginning.

'Occasionally, people like you from both north and south have joined us. Apart from this, year by year, our numbers deplete. None of us has children. Many can't, none of us wants to. We are a floating community of finite life. That's what we want to be. You will find that this makes everything very different here, if you stay.

'You will find, for instance, that we speak very little. There's no need. Perhaps you will be lonely, and miss the world you grew up in. Perhaps you will be bored. Perhaps you will find us unambitious, perhaps cold. Perhaps frightening. We know things you don't. We slip between the Force all our lives and so we have to understand them. You were near a blast. The blasts are not tests, they are a spectacle, a demonstration. The Force grow restless. It's not sanctioned, but a blind eye is turned, provided they keep it within bounds. No one sees, no one is hurt. Today, I think, they were careless of the wind.'

'That's what H said,' I interrupted, but she ignored me, as if once started she had to finish.

'I think, with the blasts, the Force tell themselves where they come from and what they serve. They inspire and entertain themselves. They tell a kind of truth. It's understandable. . . . We know this by observation as well as intuition. You will see and hear. We know there are no tests as such. We know there are things far worse than weapons hurtling unseen in the sky, and hidden in rusting bunkers. We know all this and we have no consolation.'

That's it, I thought. There is no consolation. It didn't seem frightening at all. It seemed like a heavy weight lifted from my shoulders.

'The peoples of the world who live on dry land, with four walls about them, are the children of deceitful parents. Here, we float. We live in finite time, we will dwindle and disappear. In a way we are free, but at the same time we're fugitives. We don't have any choice, but you will choose whether or not you stay with us. We hope you will.'

'I do,' I said.

'Wait a little. Sleep well. And thank you,' she added. 'I enjoy the opportunity to speak.'

I lay down next to H, washed, tended, shaved, who was still unconscious, and dreamed of the gasp of breath before impact, hit, kicked, falling, saved only by the click of a shutter in his mind. Speaker said he would live, and I believed her. Voices rang in my ears, fading and receding. The last fires spat and sighed as they were doused with salt water, slowly the figures on the wall sank into darkness. No one spoke, each lay down, alone on the rock.

In the control room on Island Paradise, the director speaks live on teleset to the leader of the World Council. Her hair is pasted across her forehead, her face hollow.

'There's been a disaster – I lost contact with the plane in mid-ocean. It failed to re-route for the Golden Desert. I think there has been some kind of equipment failure.' She doesn't avoid his eyes, though her face is heavy with guilt. Teleset is different from being really seen, face to face. His gaze, however, flickers momentarily downwards, as if discovered.

'Under the circumstances,' she continues bravely, 'I thought it best to inform the Council before issuing alerts.'

'Do nothing,' he says. 'The disaster will be announced in due course. Keep things running smoothly. There must be no more disruption. Wait for the next flight to arrive and resume your normal role.' Will she be punished or rewarded for what she's done? It's certain she can't be ignored. She presses the replay button to study his face for clues – but nothing remains: record has been jammed. She gets up and locks the door, then falls asleep across her desk.

I see the plane resting on the seabed, Holiday Flights Inc. emblazoned in gold on its side. One of its wings, broken sheer, has ploughed into the soft mud and stands upright like a memorial column. Inside the plane, bubbles strain inside small sealed cavities. The pilot has exhausted the pocket of stale air that's sustained him; it too lasted longer than he expected, and tortured him with hope.

The sea and sky are separate again. The orange life-jackets spread further and further apart, like a handful of crumbs tossed on the water. All but one are uninflated, empty, sink within the hour.

Floating

Someone from Age Counselling called and slipped a second card through the door. Come and talk with us. Confidential. I stood quietly until she went away. I guess they got the old woman I saw that time. It doesn't bear too much thinking of. I don't expect it was Martina anyway. I watched the deliverer of the card stand straight-backed by the lift, and then step inside. I congratulated myself on my quick thinking in not answering the ring. *I'd* slip through the net, I thought. Times are changing; there's something other on Three. Somehow it makes me feel stronger, almost invincible. Only a few days later, at night, I heard the lift, got out of bed and went to the door without dressing.

'You're drunk,' I muttered as I opened it, but it wasn't H: a woman in a red fashion flightsuit with tight fair curls wreathing her unlined face stood on the threshold. Eyes, the very palest green. Freckles. Her cheeks glowed with health. She scarcely noticed my accusation.

'Pardon. Can I come in?' She showed me her ID. Age Counselling.

'As you see, I was in bed.'

'An appointment –'

I went to see her today, I couldn't get out of it. That's not strictly true. I could have refused to go, as some do; that would have meant waiting until eventually they came to help me under one pretext or another – dribbling on a public bench, pushing at a crossing. . . . I suppose I could have escaped, or tried to; after all, we managed the first time, for a while at least. But the truth is, I've laid my bed here. If I manage the appointments carefully, I may still have enough time.

The office, tucked away behind Contracts, was softly lit, quite bare. She put me in the most comfortable chair. There was nothing to look at, no photographs, like Martina said she had. It was a difficult session. I said little; after all, I am not the woman on the record and I did not want to give myself away. Some of the questions she asked me were tempting.

'Have you lived a useful life?' she asked. 'Do you have a sense of satisfaction?' You are supposed to answer yes, and I wanted to, I really did, because I do have at least the beginnings of a sense of satisfaction, but, for the sake of time, I said I didn't know. She said we would work on this. She had a very sympathetic smile: she pulls her cheeks up into tight balls, but keeps her eyes wide open, staring meltingly into my eyes. Several times she took my hand briefly in hers, looked at it, then up at my face as if I was a lover; die for me, she seemed to be asking, die for me.

She said that understanding myself as part of a larger whole and a continuous progress would enable me to let go of life at the proper time. She asked me: 'Are you afraid of death?' and here, though I am not sure, I answered yes. She told me that Timely Death is never painful, and I wanted to shout, whose time though, whose time? Instead, I looked at her with what I imagine was an expression of abject hope. However, there was an answer to my unvoiced question.

'Timely Death means death in *your* time,' she said, 'but we people are not so different from each other. We all stay nine months in the womb, we mature at roughly the same rate, we discover and fulfil our life's ambitions, give or take a few years at certain times of life; we rest a little, take stock, and then we die, again, more or less at a certain age. Sometimes there are problems: problems of resolution or acceptance, some little thing that holds us back. We look back at the world which is always new, always changing, which has outgrown us, and instead of feeling a little tired, a little apart, we feel that we want to stay –'

I nodded. *We feel that we want to see it change, we feel that we want to see proof, confrontation, proclamation, a declaration of war*. She smiled. A woman who enjoys her work, I thought.

'With you, a mother, and someone who has enjoyed many years of retirement, I am sure it can only be a very little thing that holds you back.' Then she read me a poem, which referred to bees, their labours, their sense of purpose, and their painless Timely Deaths. It omitted to mention either insecticide or the queen. *Who's the queen? Who's got the honey? Who does the killing?* And unfortunate, too, that generations of bees build more or less the same thing time and time again. And then again, that there aren't many bees left. True enough, a poem to make you want to die. Or kill.

'I need time to think about all this,' I said.

'Of course,' she replied. '*Your time.*'

Not much of it. She gave me another appointment.

Afterwards, this afternoon, I wept in the street during the announcements, and people stared. I wept out of frustration, because I don't know what's happening and might die before I do. What about the something else on Three? I need the announcers to tell me, but they only tell me bits, huge intervals between; I seize on things, trying to put them together, but I still don't know what's happening. And today we saw the unveiling of a monument to commemorate the first hundred and twenty-six of Three's Untimely Dead. How many have there been since? A young man with a telescope pointing at the sky. Very muscular, a god of sorts. And they said that people working in inessential domestic chemical and engineering plants would be transferred to space, where they are needed. Matter of fact.

'We are at war,' I say to myself, 'we must be.' But it hasn't been announced, and no one else seems to care.

Time Now, and no one cares. Again:

> Yesterday, the search for the IF vessel *Esperance* was abandoned. She had been out of radio contact for ten days. Weather conditions were good, but freak storms are suspected. . . .

Another disaster; I think, what's the rationale for what we're told? Where was the *Esperance*? Doing what? Was she in Paradise region? Though I listen to the announcements every day I'll never find out. But I wonder if she was where we were, and if the floating people saw her on their stolen trackers, heard her on their radio, or someone like them if they're gone.

Each morning I woke to the sight of the floating people washing their overalls in the shallow sea that lapped at the mouth of the cave. The sun never entered the cave directly, but it was bright outside. I attended to H, washed him, gave him the food prepared daily by the man with the limp. We exchanged a nod or a smile as he gave it me, but no speech.

Then we listened in to the Force's manoeuvres, and their gossip. Rather like the announcements, except that we weren't supposed to hear. Things we never hear about here. I couldn't believe what the floating people had: a huge bank of equipment carefully stored under tarpaulins. Telescreen, receivers, trackers, aerials. The same woman always tuned in, the same bent old man patiently angled the aerials at the mouth of the cave. It took a while, the volume of interference rising and falling, sometimes difficult to distinguish from the sea. We gathered round and waited. All at once a voice would erupt, and then vanish as she fine-tuned it in. Everyone moved nearer, though in fact the voice was painfully loud, startling in the habitual silence. On the telescreen a jungle of wandering lines would appear, resolving into a map of the archipelago. As they gave their positions to the controller; these appeared as blinks of light on our monitors, and these, determining as they did any possible movement by the floating people, were carefully recorded.

'Where does all this come from?' I whispered to Speaker that first morning, but she placed her finger over her lips. That day we heard them talk about us.

'Nice little bang. Happy?'

'Happy enough,' came the reply in a slow drawl, stoned or drunk, 'but the wind blew it all over the place. That lot on Paradise might get a bit of a suntan ... ought to be more careful. . . .'

'It'll shake down, what can they do? Spotted a yacht of all things. Picked up some man who said he was sailing the ocean single-handed. Off his head. Dried up bit of skin and bone. They did him in, dumped him on the island and set it alight. Blew a hole in the yacht.'

Their laughter battered the walls of the cave, distorted, demonic.

'Some have all the chances. I'm so bored I could fuck a shark.'

'Shouldn't be bored. I'm not bored. We've got the blasts now and then. Biggest thing there is. Could be a lot, lot bigger, a real one. It'll be needed one day whatever they say . . . they *know* or else why don't they stop it? Ought to get into space if you're bored, quite a life I'm told . . . hey, heard the one about the pygmies?'

'What?'

'They say this part of the world is swarming with pygmies in canoes, nipping in and out of the islands so quick we never get a beep of them . . .'

The volume control had been broken; all this boomed around us, oppressively loud. We tuned into Forecast:

> Paradise: satellite reports of large static cloud masses, shedding dust, picked up by high winds in the Golden Desert region. Scattered showers. Region to reopen to sea and sky traffic at noon. Starship, Unity Northwest . . .

We switched to the announcements, sound only:

> . . . was lost in space three days after launch. Experts are investigating technical failures. A new holiday zone was opened in the north polar region. The Palace of Ice and Fire offers spectacular atmospheric and scenic effects as well as all the most modern . . .

'What can we do?' I said to Speaker, reluctant to break the silence of the others, whom I'd never yet seen speak. She looked puzzled.

'We can do nothing,' she said.

On the morning of the third day, H regained consciousness with a piercing scream. The transmitter was emitting its blows of sound and information, waves hissed on the back rocks, and above it all his scream fell and swooped without pattern, without even the rhythm of breath. I ran to him and held him with my eyes shut, as if that would protect us from the battering of sound. My arms about him pulled tighter and tighter, as if to squeeze the noise out of him. Then I realized several people were engaged in loosening my grip, and I let go. The scream stopped. We were the centre of a crowd, all crouched or bent to watch us. They smiled as they stared. Their smile was for H, his recovery, but caught me at its edges. Someone leaned forward to pick up the pieces of a bowl that had been broken, then carried them carefully to add to a row of other broken objects. Speaker sat next to H.

'I am Speaker,' she began, 'I will tell you who we are . . .' The speech had already bitten into my memory, and I felt the ripples of each succeeding phrase pushing at those next to be spoken. I felt the cave we were sitting in was the real centre of the world, and I clapped my hands, thud thud, along with the rest. But when H's turn came to speak, he closed his eyes and turned his head away.

Sometimes a shoal of dolphins came to the mouth of the cave. Some of the floating people joined them, and the water, quite calm elsewhere, became a churning mass of moving bodies, waves, troughs, spray. Then they would let their voices out, not words but laughter, whistles, calls. H is right that I was besotted, and all along still looking for an island paradise. (Am I still?) It seemed to me that they exactly fitted the space they were in, satisfying its requirements, expressing it as a map expresses the pattern of a city. The water clung to their skin, collected, ran down and back. They wove between each other and the twisting fish. They slipped in and out of water and air, they were a floating community of finite life, they knew where they stood, they didn't need to speak.

'I want to stay,' I said.

'I can see,' said H. He sat propped against the cave wall. He looked terrible, his skin was lightening, the blue-black of bruises melting into yellows, browns and purple. As soon as he was better, I thought, I'd feel free to move from group to group of the floating people, getting to know their faces and functions, and I would join them in the sea when they swam.

'I haven't much choice myself,' he said, 'like this. I suppose they're better than the open sea. Sit down next to me.'

I felt embarrassed to be so close. Already I wanted space around me, and found it hard to speak at length. And somehow H seemed a stranger. Speaker watched us. Her eyes were flecked, specks of iridescent colour dispersed in pale, slightly clouded green.

*

Speaker gave H the name *Mechanic* when he succeeded in repairing the generator and improved the quality of the reception equipment. I, on the other hand, had no function-name to distinguish me; like many of the floating people, I had no name at all. Even though he had been cared for, admitted, named, H refused to belong; his relentless curiosity about the sources of their equipment seemed like suspicion, and suspicious. I felt him sitting behind me and the hairs on the back of my neck rose. I moved to sleep away from him, but he followed me.

I rowed well, the overalls straining across my back. My shoulders were growing broader, my speech less frequent and more considered. I had swum with the dolphins. At night there was a small space to either side of me, even when we slept in close rows in the boats; I lay on my back, absolutely still. H said that I slept with my eyes open. Plagued by dreams, he himself slept little.

H was too weak to take an oar, and sat next to the equipment. I guessed that he was thinking the thoughts he whispered to me at night before I slept.

'*My time,*' he'd whispered in the night, '*will be as brief as the closing of a shutter. One moment, when I will have the choice.*'

I'd pretended to be asleep.

Speaker came, as she often did, to sit with H.

'You're almost recovered now,' she said. 'Do you still have bad dreams?'

'Not often,' said H, though his dreams – sagas of staccato violence played out to the whining of radio interference and laughing soldier voices on the air – came nightly, and grew nightly longer and more elaborate. He would wake, sometimes grasping my hand, sweating, the moment before the blow landed, the flames bit, the moment before death. But they were not *bad dreams* any more, they were his. He expected them.

'We will need fuel soon,' he suggested bluntly; he

wanted to know where it came from. Quiet, quiet, I thought, wait, there's no need to ask.

'Mechanic,' said Speaker softly, as if it was a beautiful name, then paused, gathering her words together. 'In the archipelago are two vanishing islands. One is a volcano which sinks below the sea in the space of forty years or so; it disappears before soil has time to settle, and then later it returns quite suddenly, larger or smaller, a little to the north or south of where it was before. I have seen it once. It has never been charted.'

H looked away impatiently. 'I'm sick of your stories,' he said.

Speaker took hold of his arm. 'Listen. The other island is also uncharted, though once it was. It has a fine harbour with no reefs or shallows, large enough to take tankers and the smaller military ships. Once it was the most densely populated island in the archipelago. The soil was fertile, there were towns and villages scattered among well-tended fields of fruit, vegetables and corn: seen from the air it was a patchwork of brilliant colour. The islanders lived on what the soil produced, they lived like part of the land itself; time wound back to its beginning every year, and there was no word for war but many words for god. Then people came who said there was one word for god and a hundred kinds of war; the island people grew sick and their language grew confused, then died.

'Now, that island's soil is dust, its towns razed; it is the International Force's ocean stores, living proof that there are a hundred ways of war. Its heart has been dug out and filled with a concrete store for fossil fuels, equipment and extinct weaponry.

'Mechanic. You need to know everything. You need to disassemble us and then put us together again. You need to know the weight of each part and how we work.'

'Yes,' H whispered. My skin pricked as at danger. I wished he wasn't there.

'Listen,' said Speaker, drawing closer. 'We go by night

and take from them our fuel and supplies; and each time we also take one of the smaller items of weaponry. A canister, of virus, explosive, fusion material, poison gas . . .'

I pulled steadily on my oar, listening. I glanced at the others about me; their faces showed only the effort of rowing, the pleasure of missing a few strokes now and then, to rest in the sun. Speaker's words spilled on, unstoppable; words are dangerous, I thought. Speaker, you're using too many; silence suits us better.

'What d'you do with it?' interrupted H. Speaker sighed.

'Nothing,' said Speaker. 'There is no consolation. In the beginning, we hoped to take it all. But though our caves are stacked high, many times more remains. We know we will never possess it all. Our takings are so small a proportion that there is scarcely any danger that they will be noticed. We learned that what we are trying to take outnumbers us, just as it will outlive us.'

'Why do you do it?' said H. 'It's useless.'

'It's better in our keeping. We understand it, it's in our bones. We rescue. We intervene. We have defused mines and other weapons. We have caused failures publicly attributed to leaks, erosion and human error. We have prevented and spoiled blasts. We keep the materials we have taken in the same spirit. We keep them for our own benefit. You will come to see in time.'

He won't, I thought. I began then to hate him, sensing he would spoil it all, that calm rhythm of rowing in the bright shadow of death. His voice, insinuating, insidious, but Speaker wouldn't know how to read it: 'Can't you do more?'

'We're surrounded by the IF. We have no official existence. We live in a hidden space and we are small; we are like an egg spinning next to a sun. If we speak, we are dead. We do what we can.'

H was thoughtful. He avoided my glare. I rowed steadily, the muscles round my neck tightening, my throat dry. Not long ago, I'd lived in Dove City and worked in light tech; I'd sat on a shelldust beach and tried to dream of elsewhere. Elsewhere. Here.

'Mechanic,' said Speaker, touching H's knee, 'I'll keep you close. Where your thoughts differ from ours is a spark. We're finite, but not fixed. You may bring us closer to ourselves.' She paused, as if there was an alternative she did not want to suggest.

'You may change us,' she concluded quietly. Her eyes were lowered, her body loose, her face lightly glazed with sweat. Her voice had the heavy, distended quality of one labouring under the burden of a secret love. H sat rigid like a statue. I was afraid, my oar slipped in my hands, the blade skated and bounced across the water.

We listened every day to the Force's channel. As a result of H's efforts, the voices of the IF controllers were crystal clear. Now, I could readily distinguish them one from another: the one that always told stories, the coward, the joker. They had an easy familiarity with the illegal and unspeakable, and were not at all like the people back home; here.

'"Anyway," I said, "do that again and you're lost overboard like the last one –"'

'Remember this is an accessible channel –'

'Who gives a damn? Did you hear about D35?'

'There isn't a D35.'

'But there used to be. They say she was lost at sea. But this is what really happened: they were stuck at the South Pole, nothing but white, water and ice. They went through the usual things – trials, films, ran out of you know what and ended up eating each other. There was plenty of food. They did it for fun. Daily lottery. No ranks excused.'

'Dog eat dog.'

'Woof. Take my advice, kid, and get into space. That's where it'll really happen. Where it's ticking. No silly games up there. Anyway, here's your real news: there's going to be another blast but we're not in on it. And D16 reckon they've lost one somewhere, so we've got to go and look for it. . . .'

'The blind listening to the mad,' H commented, as he packed the aerials away. The old man had died, and been set to sea on a burning canoe. For several days after, no one left the cave.

I was jealous sometimes of Speaker's evident love for H, and frightened by it, because there seemed to be no other such bonds among the people. At the same time, H clung to me as he had never done before. 'Where are you going?' he'd ask, and even though I didn't answer, he'd make sure to be on the same boat as me when we went to gather wood, fish or food. My shadow, H. My flesh crept. His broken body and what seemed like a torrent of words revolted me. 'Laurie, are you awake?'

'Laurie, speak,' his hand on my arm, his small hunched figure, always near.

We were making the long journey to Force's Island, made longer by the need to circumvent the Force. Sometimes we had to travel in the opposite direction for days on end. We camped on a beach plagued with flies and ants. The roar of the surf sounded strangely dry in the distance, like particles of grit rotated inside a metal drum. Everyone was lying face-down, trying to sleep in the day. A strong warm wind blew, lifting our hair and puffing up our overalls. For the first time since we had arrived, I sensed tension amongst the floating people, ostensibly at rest.

'They have never used what they know or have,' H whispered to me, scandalized, venomous.

'Don't whisper,' I answered, loudly, as I always did, 'there's nothing need be secret.'

'I hate it here! I hate it wherever we are, with them. They're all just waiting to die. They don't even try,' he said. 'I will. I can. I will blow it open and afterwards whatever's left will be true.'

I've kept from our time with the floating people a desire to give my life the proper shape for the place it grows in, even if I would rather it was a different place and the growth freer. Even if I haven't the tools to do it, that's what I want. Even so, H says that I have delusions of grandeur. He's blind to the irony.

Sometimes I accuse him of self-deception. 'You're motivated by ordinary twisted love, nothing special.' I've said often, 'I thought you'd take me somewhere but you never wanted to go anywhere but back to the same place . . . look at us, here.'

'I've hated more than loved,' he'll answer, dourly.

'What's new?' I say, 'what's different? Everyone's like that, groping for truth in strange ways, tearing at the flesh of their nearest and dearest in the hope of finding something hard to hold. You're only like everyone else. So am I.'

'I killed Jo,' he says, something like an edge of a threat to his voice.

'So?' I say. 'You haven't killed me yet. Once you drew me like a magnet, but I know you're made of ordinary metal. I'll stay or go of my own choice.'

'Where would you go? You'd've never gone anywhere without me –' he begins, angrily, but then his face crumples like paper and he says, 'Don't go . . .'

'Maybe.'

It's awful. We struggle for power. Without his self-deception H would have none, he'd be a handful of guts. Without my delusions of grandeur I would be a scattering of iron, drawn this way, then that.

We rowed in the night. It was humid, the moon indistinct. The receiver was on and tuned; somewhere a Forceman had left his set on and we heard him humming in snatches, out of tune, half-forgotten themes. I found myself crying a little, because I recognized some of the tunes, recalled their full and pure sound; their confident movement was the essence of a former life.

Apart from this, we travelled some hours in silence, until the smooth profile of the Force's Island appeared, an even curve rising out of the water like a woman's breast.

'See it?' H said, and I turned to touch his hand.

From there, we let the wind and current take us in. We sat with our heads tilted back to look at stars that were dim, as if shining through greased glass. This was a journey the floating people had made times without number: the steerers were redundant.

Speaker's voice, like a hand reaching through thick velvet curtains, parted the silence. Although we could all hear, she addressed herself to H. She spoke not simply to inform, but also it seemed, as some kind of gift.

'Tonight, I am the collector of weaponry. It is the hardest task. Mechanic, you can come with me if you wish, follow me exactly through corridors below the soil of a dead island that once lived, and carry the same weight as me, if you can bear it. You will see.'

As if a shutter had fallen, I see us, as in reality I could not. The fleet of small craft drifting on flat, black water towards the glimmer of a shore. In one of them, the largest, the one that carried, our stolen ears and eyes, I see Speaker gazing at H, pulling her features out of the darkness into sight that feels like touch. H is remote. I am invisible. We are doomed. Night, water. Strokes of the oar. Again that triangle, me watching. The first time was in the bright of morning, the table glaring white, Jo's fingernails were painted silver, scratch, scratch at the blistered table-top, and her hair shone in the sun, the bruise showed through; I listened, she died and we escaped.

I knew why Speaker broke the usual bounds of her speech. What it was that made her abandon her careful emphases and repetition. Why her words as she went on seemed to creep and multiply of their own will. Because once I had wanted H to see me with his stern and powerful eyes, glass and flesh, that bent the light to a burning spot, that picked out the essence, the moment before dissolution.

I felt suspicious and jealous of H.

I gave myself at that moment a name on behalf of the floating people: Watcher. I carry it still, though I've left them behind.

We reversed our overalls so that we did not reflect light. We gathered in a line on the thin shore. The whole of the floating people, the fit, the lame, the old, burning inside. H stood next to Speaker. We let go of each other's hands and then moved apart until we were alone. A halo of wispy clouds hanging round the dull moon gathered into one and carefully obliterated it. We began to move forwards, our empty boats on the sea behind, a skyline, half-imagined, half-hoped, in front. We walked alone so as not to leave a path over the years.

Damp sand, and then dry, became stone and plant felt underfoot. I could see nothing, nothing, there was no reason for eyes. I felt myself reeling over invisible abysses; I couldn't stand, I crawled so as to see with my hands as well as my feet. I was on an uphill slope strewn with flat pieces of stone like soft slate, smaller and smaller pieces crumbling in my hands; then the slope was pure dust and my feet sank, buried and slipping. When I paused I could feel the dust settling on my skin, touching me like someone's breath, but dry. And then my hands struck rough pebbly concrete that was warm to the touch, fragmented in places as if the ground had moved beneath it, slabs of irregular shape and torn edges, with twisted steel rods and small thorny plants thrusting through cracks. The thorn plants came thicker; no choice but to tread on thorns, the thin sharp pain like blades of light in the dark, almost welcome.

I walked on alone through waist-high bushes with papery whispering leaves, I blundered into sudden outcrops of warm rock. I ached in the small of my back, the backs of my thighs. I longed for the touch of human flesh, for the sound of my own voice, someone else's, H. Suddenly I was striding on smooth ground, ordinary soil, I felt a wind part to pass me, join again behind. It smelled of burnt dust. I opened my eyes as I crept over the crest of the hill, and paused to listen. There was no sound but the wind dividing itself to encompass small projections of rock, fragile tufts of plant, dividing itself just as it did to pass me, following my shape, resealing itself; and for the first time I felt that the others were there, the silence was human and it confirmed their presence.

The other side of the hill was wet. Succulents grew on the upper slopes, crushing coolly underfoot. The soil was thick and damp, the air rich with half-heard water sounds, drips and trickles, the rising and turning of mist. Sweat collected on my skin. I resisted gravity, the urge to loosen my thighs and calves and run. So downhill was a dull ache of control, and the darkness growing denser. Sharp wet grasses, crushed, pressed aside and springing back like whips. My feet peeled carefully from the half-liquid earth to prevent the sudden breaking of suction. The slope eased. I stood straight with no fear of falling, I walked steadily forward and forgot in the walking why I was there.

The first tree grazed my arm. I stood still and someone took my hand. Her touch did not startle me. She gave me a rough coral bead and ran the empty string through my fingers: I was the last.

⋆

And that same night, in darkness like ours, I see and feel the bartender pitch and wallow in the sea. The absolute brightness of day, the utter dark of night, an alteration as unerring as that of the crests and troughs that spit him up, then swallow him down. He prefers night to day, for then his thirst subsides and his eyes can no longer scan the horizon or search the sky. Sometimes he even sleeps. Sometimes the waves wash over him in his sleep and he wakes choking but floating again, carried by the air inside the orange life-jacket. Though he's made no attempt to swim or steer himself and has no idea which way he's moving or if at all, warm currents are carrying him steadily on; and though deadly biting fish, their bodies knit from strands of tempered muscle, their skins like sandpaper, swim below his dangling feet, they pass him by and thrust steadily on: driven by the clocks and maps and memories in their cells to breed, they are swimming against the current that carries him on, carving their path back home.

For a few seconds the air around me seemed alive with movement. I could see nothing. It was still again. Then someone guided me under the fence. We crawled on our hands and knees. I don't know who I was with, I didn't ask questions. We filled our packs with tubes of ointment, penknives and overalls, packed tight into balls no bigger than a fist. I grabbed too fast, and a hand restrained me. I was terrified, blind with fear to be in such a place.

Speaker took H's hand and broke the silence.

'Mechanic,' she whispered, 'can you hear it?' A thin hum pitched just within hearing, and, fainter still, a rapid, hollow clicking.

'Are you afraid?'

'No,' H said, but the word lost itself in his mouth, emerged as a fragment of breath. Speaker pressed him to the ground.

'Keep down. They use electric eyes. . . . Can't you feel

it? Don't move. Don't touch. Can't you feel it?'

They stand in the most contained space on earth, beneath steel, water, concrete, and lead layered like the hard shell of our planet itself.

'Mechanic, can't you feel it?'

Material power buried, compressed yet seeping into the motionless atmosphere like the distant song of slaves with a will to be free. Could they feel themselves burning ever so slightly, the hair on their arms and legs twisting and scorching, the water in their eyes drying away?

Speaker pulls H to her and holds him, their bodies pressed tight.

'Mechanic, oh Mechanic, what will –' she begins. The space around them hums and festers; in time it could turn everything to matter, their poor flesh, water, mineral, so essentially mutable; their bodies held human only by the attraction of opposites and something inside that's heating and slowly softening like a coil under charge.

H breaks away from Speaker. 'Hurry. Let's do what we came for. I want to get out!'

Trembling, Speaker slides out a rack of canisters. Does she know what she's doing?

'These are the smallest.'

The container is tubular, smooth and cool, coated in seamless lead. H's hands could find no grip on it. Speaker, pushing him aside, lifted it enough to slip the straps of a harness beneath.

'Here,' she whispers, loading it on to H's shoulders.

'So what happened?' H asked me.

'When?'

'What happened with the Age Counsellor?'

'I told her I was afraid to die. She said Timely Death meant death in my time. I've got to go again.'

'Don't –'

'No. Not yet. Talk to me.'

'No.'

I got out some paper and a pencil.

'What's this in aid of? '

'Draw something then,' I said. 'The first thing that comes into your mind.'

'Nothing does.'

'Try.'

After a while, he drew the outline of a person, then added a halo of scribbled curls.

'Jo?' I asked, and leaned forward to add a hole in the side of the head. He snatched the paper away.

'No! It's no one. You do one.'

I scribbled quickly. Random, I thought, but it was a map of Island Paradise. I added some sea, choppy little waves in blue. He laughed.

'More?' I felt quite excited.

'No. Another time perhaps.'

'Too much for you? Time for a drink?' What makes him so precious. On the other hand, why be churlish? It's better than before: progress! There are six pencils and I keep them always in a neat row on the window-sill. If one goes missing, if he does any more, I want to see them. He used to take pictures; now he can draw them. He took pictures of Jo and then shot her with air. I feel it's my right to see.

The Enemy

Our blue-eyed president declared today that we have no choice but to take an aggressive position *vis à vis* whatever it is that wants Three. There is no alternative to Three, or none sufficient. If we let Three from our grasp, all our achievements would be lost, and we would live as in the darkest of the past. He is sure we do not need reminding, but all the same . . .

We see pictures of Time Before. There are still no pictures of whatever it is that also wants Three, but for the first time today – when I was supposed to go to Age Counselling but didn't – it has been called the Enemy. A word we'll have to practise saying: E-ne-my. Enemy means the bodies of our workers, hanging on strings or lost in space. Enemy means the indoor air feels cold and we sometimes sit in the dark at night. The lightshows are closed, the traffic signals erratic. Enemy means young people sucked to Untimely Deaths in space. But Enemy means more than that. Enemy: I say it softly to myself, it's a musical word, all vowel; gentle, the Enemy. The Enemy sounds like seas, calmly changing shape. The Enemy is a sense that everything might not go on as before. I think I half love the faceless Enemy; I wonder, will they rescue me?

Perhaps there are no pictures of the Enemy because they look like us. Perhaps there is no Enemy. Perhaps they are us, or some of us. Suppose. Suppose some of us are being sent to fight others of ourselves, on behalf of yet others.

Suppose there is no Price to pay, not to anyone else. Suppose we need not. Suppose we need not die. I wish I could live for ever, just to see –

'Stop it!' H's voice tears. I've made H shout, spin away, hands over ears. I shout back.

'What do you think? Who are *you* paying to, for what you did? Who's paying for you? And who would have paid for what you nearly did as well? It's me, isn't it? Suppose I stop, damn you, suppose I stop?' I enjoy it, the words tearing the soft skin of my throat, my face scalding crimson.

'You keep away from me,' commands H, voice almost even again. He picks the games terminal from the floor, brushes his finger over its dust and begins to uncoil the lead.

'No! We don't use that!' I say, and cross the space between us and take hold of his face by the chin. I can feel the bone, sharp, uneven; there it is again: I could kill. I'm on my own. What have I got to lose? Slowly, cooling, I let go. He puts the terminal down.

'And who's paying for you to sleep like a baby night on night?' I add, under my breath, 'I am sick of keeping you safe,' but not ready, not quite, to stop. 'You make me sick,' I say.

Though we have tried long and hard to maintain our position on Three by means of defensive tactics alone, says blue eyes, we are suffering unacceptable losses. I want to see its face, the Enemy's, not his. We've seen its fire now, strange streaks of light and silent explosions that eventually obscure their own image with dust, fade themselves out. And we've seen the bodies in close up, though none as yet has been carried home. It's strange to think, among the stars and planets, our Untimely Dead are whirling in the sky. And the Enemy, I think, how many of them have died? Thousands? Millions? None? Perhaps there is no Enemy. Perhaps there is only one. Suppose.

> Some of us will have friends or colleagues who have been killed Untimely by the Enemy. And these are young people, our hope for time to come. Before long, if we do not act, there will be empty chairs all about us, and silent work-places as well as dark nights. The Enemy has no scruples.

Again, we see its escalating damage – a halo of debris whirls around Three, a strange light hovers, flickers, the picture breaks into wavy lines, returns, disappears –

> It is with the greatest reluctance but also a kind of pride that the Council have decided that we must take aggressive action. For is not our peaceful and progressive way of life worth preserving against an Enemy that, with streaks of fire, wreaks Wilfully Inflicted Untimely Death and sabotages our enterprise with barbarous bombs long since abolished here? The Enemy has no scruples, he will take from us everything we have, including life.
>
> Our course of action must be to eliminate the Enemy.
>
> In the months to come I will be asking of you great sacrifice, great courage; the struggle is far away, but will be fierce.

After his speech, we see our beautiful earth shining green and blue, trailing mists. We get closer, and closer, as if soon it will show us ourselves, looking up. Our own image, to frighten us. More memorials have been unveiled. But still he hasn't called it a *war*.

The thought of a war excites me, although I don't exactly want it. But now that my terrible dreams seem to be coming true, I do not need to have them. I feel clearer, healthier and more courageous.

If there is to be a war, I want to know. I will be glad for the knowing, not for war. Unless they lie. Perhaps lying is already a kind of war. I tell myself it may not happen.

Tonight, the power cuts are worse, half the town is dark. I try to imagine the Enemy's face, but it may not even have one and I can't. Eliminate – that's another new word with an old sound. I shall climb in beside H and hold him to me. He's been my enemy, in the past. H for Haley, which he doesn't like, H for Him. I've never forgiven. I'll wrap my cold heavy flesh round him, match my breathing to his, even though tonight the floating people seem closer than him, lying within reach. With the insistent pressure of my body against his, my hand seeking parts of him that are alert even in sleep, I could wake him. It was because of H that I lost the floating people. H is a destroyer. H has inflicted Untimely Death, at least once. I am close to him. Once I thought he was some kind of answer and I was wrong. I sleep next to him every night, and I would miss him if he wasn't there. H is the enemy. And so what am I? I've *kept him close*, as Speaker said. But it's not loyalty, it's a task. Nightly I've marked his neck with water and held him to me, a burning, fighting, obliterating thing. A bomb, ticking away. I've cut myself away from everything else. It's me, and him. It's me and a killer. It's me and a bomb. I could wake him. I could kill him.

But I shan't. I'm tired, and hope I will sleep. I'm old. I am taking him apart so he won't work again. I've had to love him, but I mustn't pay the Price.

It's cold now, so cold. Our breath turns to frost on the window. That's never happened before. I play with pictures in my mind. I see sunrise at Paradise Island, the glittering green, the sun-spangled sea, vivid in its beauty, complete in its deception. I open my eyes, there's darkness about me, and quiet, just as then, and in the middle of the dark are Force's stores, ticking over, waiting for their time.

As we descended the dry slope of Force's Island we saw something that must be the sea, a faint shine below, like a mirror crusted with centuries of dust. And then we could see the smudges of shadow that were each other, and our bodies were released from the burden of care and silence and we began to run downhill, our packs crashing into our backs, sliding, falling and saving ourselves until we came to the beach, which was covered by the morning tide, sweeping cool about our feet, crashing about our waists. We waded to our boats and waited for Speaker and H. As the light came, we grew tense and fearful, and our silence seemed to grow stronger and heavier, as if that silence was a great strength that bound us together. And at last, bowed under the weight they carried, descending much slower than us, they came. H sat in the bows. Speaker lay her head in H's lap. We took up our oars.

The entrance to our stores was a small opening at sea-level in an island of rock. The water there was in deep shadow, icy. No weeds or barnacles grew. Each craft slowly disappeared as its crew heaved it through; then came the smell of smoke from lighted torches, and the next went in. We, with the canisters on tow, were last, slipping easily through on a surge of the rising tide.

Inside the cold was complete and sudden. We left our boats in the first chamber and progressed, uphill, on foot. We stood waist-high in water. All our faces were wet, gilded in the torchlight by streams of silent tears, which came to me sudden and unexpected.

We passed along a tunnel; the water grew shallower

and we left the boats, continuing on foot in single file, the raft and canisters bringing up the rear.

There grew among us an air of complete exhaustion and despair. Each step came unwilling but inevitable. The tunnel twisted, swallowing up the torches ahead of us. I wanted to run back into the light we had come from, but it had gone. The tunnel narrowed. I took one of the raft ropes, now dragging, now lifting the canisters along. Time and time again we grazed our skin on sharp uneven rock, banged our heads and shoulders. Our progress was so painfully slow, debilitating; it was like the end of a long illness, struggling for breath despite the desire to abandon hope.

We stumbled into a low, roughly circular cave. We stood in the middle, a flickering huddle in the swamp of darkness that surrounded us. People leaned on each other like broken dolls, their faces hung creased by exhaustion; they wept, they looked old and undone, unpicked by memory and grief. The sight of them passed through me, like acid through paper: I made my way blindly to join them.

H and Speaker carried the canisters out and away from us, until their torches lit up rock. They began to circle the cave. We at the centre turned outwards, and watched them as they walked. At their feet, a line of single canisters like those they carried lay on the ground, a brief fringe of metal radiating out like petals. About three-quarters of the way round, the row of canisters came to an end. With sharp crashes that reverberated back along the whole line, they dropped their two into place. On Speaker's instruction, H bent and scooped a handful of water from a shallow pool. Speaker dipped her fingers in it and touched their canisters. We in the centre were suddenly inflamed with a sharp and terrible fear; we pressed closer together, restraining each other, containing it. Then, one by one, we broke out of the group to follow Speaker as she completed the circuit of the cave; and as each one left it seemed that the fear wound itself tighter among those left behind, and the more we wanted to escape, the harder we clung to each other; our nails dug in, our fists tightened; arms fastened round waists, necks, legs. We wanted to run out into the sun, but the tunnel was already full and we must leave as slowly as we had come, on our hands and knees, down a narrow passage with a fading light, smoke in our lungs and hair. But it was over, until the next time. Blinking, we crawled into the daylight, lay shivering and exhausted in our boats.

I was half asleep in the sun, my limbs rocked loose. I felt the warm wood of my oar, deep-grained but smooth. It was done. I felt a great satisfaction, as if I never need move again. Something warm was placed in my lap. I kept my eyes closed. It lay there dense and insistent. Food.

Someone said, 'He's not here.'

I felt the boat lurch as Speaker stood and called to the other craft. 'Mechanic's left behind. He's in the cave. We must go back.' She repeated herself to each of the craft gathered about us. People looked up, weary, but no one put their hands to the oars. It was as if we were frozen.

'No –': a voice not Speaker's. There was a palpable sense of relief in the boat, as if we had drifted suddenly from night to day, and then others began, breaking one by one the custom of leaving all words to Speaker's care.

'He threatens us.'

'He dreams of destruction.'

Someone reached up, and guided Speaker slowly down. She sat, looking at us all, startled.

'He never wanted to stay.'

'He holds us in contempt.'

'The Force are near.'

'We never go back.'

'He whispers in the night.'

'He lies.'

'He is all our enemy.'

Their voices, so long unused, came out clear, striking home one after the other. H, a list of your sins. The things I myself had thought, as I watched you, as I pushed you away, because I wanted to stay, to enact time and time again the perfect ritual of the floating life. My legs began to shake. My heart was running away from me too fast to count; blood beat in my ears and the backs of my eyes.

'But there's no need to be afraid of him,' said Speaker, her voice rising as if to say, *Is there? Tell me there isn't –*

'Yes, there is!' I said, hoarse, and threw the warm damp package of food in my lap over the side as hard as I could. 'He killed his mother Jo.'

Speaker, silenced, covered her face with her hands, and several people moved to comfort her, even as they continued speaking.

'He would never change.'

'He had bad dreams and cherished them.'

'We'll not go back.'

We were drifting further away from the cave mouth. Like a thin sheet settling softly on our skin, silence returned. One by one the people about me took up their oars again and tried to gather themselves together, searching for the lost thread of their silence. We were leaving, and leaving him behind. The sea stretched ahead, calm, sparkling. I thought it was what I wanted, but I didn't reach for my oar. I glanced hopefully at Speaker; abject, exhausted, it seemed she had betrayed me by her defeat. All about me oars bit the water. I could still be part of that rhythm in stomach, shoulders, arms, back; stomach shoulders arms – six long strokes, taking us away. Six more.

'But we can't –' I said, standing unsteadily. There was no answer. They only spoke when they chose. They chose not. I looked from boat to boat. They leaned forwards, their heads bent low. So disparate in appearance, so united in action. They pulled back, breathing in.

'I'll go for him, will you wait?' I shouted. Again, there was no reply. Their eyes set ahead. Speaker's face was hidden. I drew breath and dived. The small boats moved smoothly on, wake crossing wake, as if I'd never been there.

I crawled back through the long reaches of the tunnel, unwilling and afraid. Something held me back from calling out to H.

In the cave a torch lay on the ground, its reservoir of fuel pooled around it and burning so fiercely that it created a draught in the dead underground air. H had dragged several canisters to the flames, and sat amongst them, peering in the flickering light as he pored over a circuit diagram and a collection of wires and components. Aware of me, he turned round and smiled broadly.

'Good,' he said. 'Help me. You're just the person.'

I didn't, though part of me strained to obedience. 'What are you doing?' I said. 'What's in those?'

'All sorts. Enough to make a bang that can't be ignored. A cocktail. You can read this sort of thing better than me. I've got up to here. It's a detonator.' He snapped some connections home.

'They wanted to leave you behind,' I said, 'but I've come to get you.'

'Won't make any difference where you are.' His fingers began their work again. I caught hold of his arms, pulling them back. I tried to drag him towards the fire. He freed himself. We were twisting and pushing, we were rolling my way, his. And then my fingers were at his throat, strong, sinking; he went limp, relaxed, he slammed his knee into my stomach. *I'll kill him*, I thought, and suddenly I was on top, I'd pinned him down, my leg jammed his against one of the cylinders, hot from the fire of the torch. All the time he was laughing, deep in his throat, then higher, as I pressed down on his chest, harder, higher, until it was only the shape of a sound, ghost of a gurgle, his lips mouthing: 'Go on then.'

I lifted his head, intending to smash it down, but at the last second I did – could – not.

'You could,' he said. I released my grip. He watched as I pulled apart his work, flung the leads about the cave, crushed the rest.

Afterwards, there was a great stillness. He didn't move. I waited for the vomit, the tears, that were stuck inside me. The fire went out. I don't know how long it was we sat in darkness in that cave, amidst the various means to mass Untimely Death, so carefully carried from one store to another. The made, as Speaker said, cannot be unmade, and now I guess they'll use them. I wondered then if the floating people knew all along what would happen. I have a feeling that they did; that they took us in their midst as they took weaponry from Force's Island, because it was there; that they sent us to our fight in the cave; that they thought, as I sometimes do, that we deserved each other. I am his keeper. I cannot change him, I cannot eliminate him; I can, if I want to, keep him safe.

We felt the walls to find our way out. The cave echoed to even the slightest sound. Of course, the floating people were gone. Vanished. The sea was empty and smooth as far as the horizon; a journey over water leaves no tracks, traces or clues, neither footprints nor scent, it closes up behind. Awash, swaying like a drunken dancer, I helped H on to the raft we had used to carry the canisters and we moved slowly away from the mouth of the cave.

The Island

A launch pad has been constructed on Force's Island. It was strange to see it, even from above. The dry side and the wet. Reassuring that we did indeed leave no path. The complex of buildings from which H and Speaker bore their canister apiece, then empty and silent, now busy with transporters and uniformed personnel.

> *We will give them what they deserve!*

Our president is there himself; we see him below the waist and wearing a suit of Force's blue. He clenches his fist, and some of the lunchtime crowd shout 'Death to the Enemy' and raise their fists, a little uncertainly, in return.

'Thank God we kept them,' someone says. 'Our weapons, I mean. After all, that's why there's no Power here, because it was used for the weapons. So now it's being used.'

'The Enemy might have something even better,' I say, boldly.

'But not so much,' I am told.

'True,' I say. *'Don't draw attention to yourself.'* That's what H tells me, when he leaves for work. *'You should get about more –'* I say, tit for tat, *'you should get yourself a camera. Everything's different.'* But, of course, he only ever took pictures of Jo. *'You shouldn't let guilt rule your life,'* I add maliciously. *'She'd've died a Timely Death by now in any case.'* Last night, I forgot to check the apartment.

We are being encouraged to waste nothing. Many of our resources are taken up with the struggle for Three.

'Our Strength is our Unity,' and the president's eyes are blue.

Clouds began to gather on the afternoon of our first day on the raft, appearing like soft padding around the horizon, darkening and solidifying as they climbed up the edges of our sky. Late on the second day, occasional drops of rain were falling, the clouds had dark purple underbellies and the sea seemed pure light: the whole sight shimmered with a strange negative glow. The sun appeared only as an ill-defined scrap of refracted light. The humid air beneath this smothering of cloud hummed with static; it was thick with trapped particles and charged waves ricocheting in the confined space between sea and sky. It was like an oven. We drenched ourselves with sea water only slightly cooler than our own sweat. The raft moved on, despite the lack of wind.

Somehow I never doubted that we would reach land, though often I dreaded it. What was ahead grew steadily larger, harder, more vivid, and more frightening. Where could we go but back? What would we do, how would we live or die? The raft itself was a haven, and H and I lay on it amidst the gathering storm in a strange kind of calm of our own, as if our fight had brought us an intimacy and a lack of fear that the escape itself, despite its promise, had not.

'That's what it's there for,' he said. 'It's there to kill as many people as possible. That's what it's kept for. What else?'

'Speaker fell in love with you just as I did. Why should we do that?'

'You both want what I wanted,' he said. He told me how, had I not stopped him making his detonator, there would be great waves washing up the sides of continents, and white dust would have fallen, thick, germ-laden, radioactive, ubiquitous. Vegetation would shrivel, rivers turn strange almost beautiful colours. The ocean fleet would be destroyed; and so would the floating people, and him, and me, and the towering cloud would pour endlessly into the sky, a dirty smoke of proof, a billowing of rage, visible.

'I don't want that,' I said. 'I wanted to stay with the floating people.'

'You could have done,' he pointed out. 'They wanted it. That's the truth,' he said, 'that stuff in the cave. I touched it. I held it.'

'It's a thing, that's all,' I said.

'No. More than a thing. Like gold was.'

Trapped there between the sluggish iron-grey sea and the clouds that thickened and seemed to grow downwards as if they had already filled all the sky above, we grew delirious. Sometimes he wept, and I put my arm round him.

'What is it?' I'd ask, laughing, as if there wasn't reason enough. 'What is it? I thought you wanted to come. D'you want to go back? Of course, I'll take you back if you want.'

We had to cling to the raft as the sea folded over us and pushed us down. The logs felt frail beneath us, they were moving at odds with each other, chafing against their ties; as we clung to it, we were also holding it together; and we felt the moving weight of water, churned and opaque, pushing into our ears and noses, and when the sea threw us up we daren't loosen our grips but lay gasping like landed fish until the next time. The sky seemed within arm's reach of the sea.

'We could just let go,' H suggested, spitting water.

'I don't want that kind of death.'

'What do you want?' – water, tons, crushing and stinging, our eyes screwed tight.

'I'd want to be very old. And you . . .' That was when

we began it, our plan, our fantasy that's no longer any use to me.

H and I, clinging to a log raft in a part of the ocean where radio signals mysteriously deflect, an island regularly sinks and rises beneath the sea, and the Force's ships steer clear. H and I, clinging to a log raft in the age of interplanetary travel, that's something. And that angry tearing wind that blew us straight on the shortest course back to Island Paradise, where there were the remains of a fire on the beach, and footprints in the sand.

I said to the Age Counsellor, quite genuinely, that I feel a great ignorance, that there is something missing which I need to know. She replied that many people need some kind of understanding in order to come peacefully to a Timely Death. She gave me a model of the carbon atom, an hour-long videogram of the planets, once called heavenly bodies: we are nearer to them now, she said.

'D'you think the world is changing?' I asked her.

'Oh, certainly,' she said, tossing her head. 'Don't let that worry you. Once progress has begun, it is unstoppable.'

'I worry that it's not changing fast enough,' I said.

'Learn to step aside,' she replied, sharply.

'Why must the old step aside?' I asked, and she turned on me.

'Because there's no room. Because they cost too much. Because they want too much and hold us back. Their thoughts go haywire, they lose their sense of purpose and their sense of place.'

'You,' she said, pointing, 'take up my space in the time to come. Do you need me to give you a history lesson? There's a price to be paid by each and every one of us. Everyone, so it's fair. We've all had the benefits. We don't want it how it was. You are the economic slack. It's in the Treaty. You're trying not to pay, you disgust me.'

I suspected this anyway, but for some reason it made me sad and tearful. Probably because of Martina, whom I've imagined changed, my friend again. It was as if she was speaking. I know she probably said the same sort of thing, and told me about it afterwards as well.

The Counsellor blushed and returned to her usual comforting manner. 'Sorry,' she said. 'I mean to say, this is not arbitrary. There is a good reason.'

I said to H, 'The thing is, I see that something's happening at last, I want to know what it is. What exactly is the battle for Three? Who is the Enemy?'

'Well, I can't tell you,' he answered. 'You're the one that studies the televideos of the World Council, the inflexions, the vocabulary, the euphemisms, you're the one that listens all night to imaginary fighting in the street. You know it won't last for ever. *Let's just do what we planned now* –'

We could have done it any time. We have everything we need. I stopped him.

He took me away from the floating people. Quits.

We've denied each other's solutions.

Saved.

Condemned.

'Please,' he said.

'Ssh –' I said. 'Look –' I pulled the curtain aside, revealing the whole rise of our white-built city, its aerials and dishes pointing at the heavenly bodies, skycraft whirling like clouds of flies around the taller buildings; below, weekend crowds gathered round street-corner televideos. Life as we know it, shimmering. Like a skin you could pierce, a rushing sound in your ears.

'So?' he said, turning away. I think he was on the verge of tears.

I go out at night now and write on the walls. I know others do the same but I never see them. *The war's not over. I'd kill to know. Island What accident?? Paradise Island, a hell on earth.* I walk past in the day and what I wrote has been erased. I write again. *Briggs – liar or fool? Karancheck – fool or liar? Time Before = Time Now. H for hypocrite.* I'm getting reckless. I pull out cables, I remove circuits from telebooths.

'How did that happen?' I ask the engineers as they mend them, and they reply 'Power fluctuation' or 'accident'. I feel bold. I go out more often, both day and night.

It's not that I want people to meet Untimely Deaths. It's not that I want war: if I had lived Time Before, I like to think I'd've been one of those people in the square, holding my banner, striking a match, knowing what the enemy was, and not alone. If there's to be death, I'd like it in a bright flame of certitude, for a reason I assented to. I don't want a war, but I'm hoping to see an end to this kind of peace.

I've been thinking: are we about to break the IF Treaty or aren't we? Spirit or letter? How long have we been doing it? How long have we not really been trying to get rid of the weapons on Force's Island, just in case. Or is it worse than that, does it go back even further?

Perhaps when Briggs, Karanchek, Minito and Ellulah met just hours after the accidental launch and its deliberate retaliation were so breathtakingly averted, they made more than one agreement. Perhaps they spent the evenings in secret huddles with their advisers, military men, manufacturers, analysts. Perhaps they didn't even quite understand the arguments – they were all very old, after all. For the comfort of the people, to stop those shrieks and cries and burnings, those refusing to work, pay taxes, those wan-faced bad-dreaming children who felt they'd nothing to lose – and to protect their security as rulers, war and weaponry must cease to be an issue. Give them what they want. Simple. But not so fast, whispered the advisers; who puts you where you are, really? Whose money keeps you ticking over? Whose technology fuels your dreams of space and stars? Your ever-onwards reason to be? Whose? Ours.

To oil economic systems, to take up the slack, to maintain the divisions and precarious balance of states, to keep what you've got, the armament industry must continue. If it does not, the advisers smiled and nodded, we might just leave you high and dry. Or worse. Let's try a compromise. Let's negotiate. Continue, but not continue. . . .

Things would have moved very fast. Like me and the Age Counsellor, they knew where they stood after that. Perhaps, leaning close as their interpreters spoke for them, their voices shaking because they knew these borrowed words would be their last, those four men agreed informally that the conflict industry must continue in secret, under other guises. Perhaps before the public treaty announced with glory and fanfare came a private agreement, a pact. Perhaps as they embraced, at midnight in a darkened room, Briggs, Karanchek, Minito and Ellulah felt like the only brothers in the world as they pitched their faith in each other against those candle-bearing hordes, as they decided it was more important to keep secrets from us than it was to keep them from each other. Or perhaps, to be charitable, they felt they had no choice.

And only after that, would they have composed the two hundred pages of the International Force's Treaty, now translated into every known language and available, bound, at every administrative office in the world. They'd've written it quickly, and with great pleasure, because it was a relief to agree for once on what was to be said, not to fight over words and undo them and recompose and throw tantrums and start all over again. A relief to say, with some degree of honesty as well, that they trusted each other, that they admired and appreciated – and such a beautiful story too: it was the pure poetry that everyone wanted to hear, and it made them into the first heroes of a new era. I envy them their story. Was it euphoria that made them boldly declare (in writing, not so loud in the speeches): *A price must be paid. Concomitant with such transformation, we shall work towards a universally reduced expectancy of longevity. . . .* Euphoria, or a simple desire to get what they could out of the situation, or even some old religious notion that no one appreciates what they've paid for? No one seems to have said, after all, why is there a price?

Or perhaps neither they nor their successors knew that the Treaty was being broken. Perhaps their good intentions were overridden, then or later. But I'm certain that there's always been preparation for war. I think we've gone looking for one, out there, in space, where none of us can properly see. I'm certain that not only has the old stuff been kept, but new things have been made, in the name of industrial progress. Look how smoothly we're sliding into battle. Look at blue eyes, raising his fist so confidently on Force's Island. Look at the way he doesn't have to explain. Look at how I feel this has all happened before.

Have we known this was coming all along? Peace was an old, old dream, and they said it had come to pass. Since then, no one's dared to shout their dreams. Have we always known our dream was murdered? Is that why we obediently take to death so young? Is that why we dream of killing, as part of us searches for the last vestiges of a power we surrendered by believing what we wanted to hear?

And who is the Enemy, who?

> Several satellite orbits have been reserved for
> special internal security purposes,

we're told this morning, huddled in the windswept and leafless square.

> The world has enjoyed over a hundred years of peace, but we must guard against the possibility, however remote, of conflict within, as well of the threat without. Our Unity is our Strength, it must be guarded. . . .

The music they play has changed as well. Instead of soaring, it thumps.

I can't prove anything. I can't sleep. There are drugs that can ease the anxiety, hints the Age Counsellor (not that I've told her what I think), and they can also bring you straight and fast to Timely Death. She's making me an offer. No thanks.

On Paradise Island's largest beach I lay, as before, in the full afternoon sun. Taking a handful of sand, almost too hot to hold, I saw that each grain of shelldust was smoothly rounded, almost spherical. I poured them on my stomach, and they caressed the skin like warm water. H lay next to me. We two were silent, we seemed to have lost the taste for words.

There were dead fish floating in the sea, approaching, receding, approaching; and others, shrunken and stiff, lay on the otherwise perfect sand. The tide had washed away all traces of the last holiday-makers, there were no footprints but our own. It seemed that the waves beat on the shore faster than before.

The bartender sat bolt upright, his back to the sea, watching us. He talked incessantly. His eyelids were puffy. A patchy beard sprouted from his chin. His hair, once thick and tidy, had thinned and grown at the same time. Bleached and encrusted with salt, it hung about his head in a flimsy mass of tangles ending in thin points where he'd wound it round and round his forefinger. As well as this, he kept pushing his feet one after the other into the sand, then pulling them alternately free, like someone running in a dream.

'I like your style,' he was saying, 'frying yourselves to death. You should keep those overalls on, that's what they're for. Been sick yet? You will be. Mind you –' he pointed at me '– you don't look so bad, you'll outlast him.' I closed my eyes and tried to ignore him.

'Can't stay here,' he said, for what seemed like the hundredth time. 'Can't stay here.'

'Why on earth not?' I answered.

'We won't last very long. Well, for one thing, the whole place was covered in white dust. After you went, before we did. Like dry snow, but hot.' He stopped talking and pulled up his tattered orange life-jacket to show me the burns and blisters below. The gesture surprised me out of an irritation with his patter that had grown almost to hatred. Sensing this, he began to weep.

I sat up and spoke patiently. 'There's no alternative. How could we go back? I'm a disappeared person. H killed his mother. We all saw too much. Especially you.'

'I'm not talking about me going back,' he said.

'Why're you so concerned about us then?'

'I don't know,' he smiled through his tears, 'but I am.'

'Listen,' I said. 'We've been close to the stuff for months. I told you. He's picked the canisters up. Maybe there's not that much of it. Anyway, going away now won't make any difference. And I don't want to go back, I couldn't bear it, I couldn't bear to be Laurie Hunter, I couldn't bear to go to work, I couldn't bear to be asked about Kim. How could we just go back?'

He tapped the side of his head, then shook it. One of his tears landed on my arm, dried instantly in the heat.

'Remember: no one but the very top knows what's really happened here. None of the Wilfully Inflicted Untimely Deaths will be recorded, of course they won't; on the record it'll be a disaster. Just a disaster. Just a couple of hundred accidental deaths. Surely that was the whole idea? Clear up all the mess in one fell swoop. Instrument failure.'

I shrugged.

'You're the one that never had daydreams, aren't you?' he said.

I didn't answer.

'If you don't want to be you, you can be the one that was shot. You can be his mother,' he said, pointing at H, who laughed.

'I don't even look like Jo.'

'People change. No one looks. A terrible ordeal, adrift for you don't know how long, starving, opening your mouth to catch the rain. You're the same size. You can have your hair done.'

'H wasn't even on the plane. Someone'll check.'

'That's a risk you take,' he said, 'or go without him. You've got to have the numbers, that's the thing. And then you say, oh what a lovely time we had, what beautiful beaches and splendid service, how lovely it was to get away, until suddenly – I can see it – the staff coped wonderfully. Front it out. You might be lucky.'

'Lucky? You're mad. I told you what happened to H. They'll just get rid of us. We can stay here. It suits me. I like it now,' I said.

'They'll be back to decontaminate. And to test. They'll go over every tree and behind every rock. No one's supposed to be here. I'd say the other way you have more of a chance.'

'We can float. We can make rafts,' I said. 'We've done that before.'

'You be Jo,' interrupted H. 'I like that idea.'

'Leave me alone,' I said.

'I want to show you something, both of you,' said the bartender. 'Come with me.'

The runway was covered with a fresh accumulation of white dust, pitted and congealed from rainfall. There were slurries of footprints, there were broad double-tyre tracks from the planes, smooth curves moving into the distance. I walked along one of them, and stood a few minutes where a plane had lifted off; the track grew suddenly faint, then stopped as if it had been cut off with a knife. Around the buildings an area had been cleared of dust. We walked through the lounge, which was immaculate, the goblets waiting in stacks on the counters, the tables clean, the bins empty. The air-conditioning was humming. A tap was running into a steel sink.

'Drinks?' said the bartender. He served them with a smile and a professional flourish at odds with the torn life-jacket hanging from his emaciated frame.

'On the house, of course.'

He took us to the office. The director, rotting, lay over her desk. The monitors had been turned off. H dropped his drink. The plastic goblet bounced gaily on the floor. He leaned on the door-frame, eyes shut, chest heaving.

'She was the one that sent the plane down,' the bartender said.

'Did you –?' H asked.

'Me? No. Maybe she did it herself. Maybe it was the dust. Maybe they sent someone, in with the next lot of paradise seekers. They were the last. Closed for environmental attention now. Preserve the beauties of the landscape, repair the damage of all those eager feet. They all had a lovely time. I watched them have it. I hid. Staring at the sea and wondering what was the matter with them. Coffee in the morning, drinks at sunset, listening to the waves, searching the sky, wishing they were dead, longing to be home. Screwing, quarrelling, wanting to kill. I hid. Funny thing, it's the women the place gets to hardest. Like you. No more have come since they went. I've drunk some liquor but I won't touch the food.'

We led H away.

'Don't think I haven't felt like killing. But it's an ignorant thing to do. The more you know, the less you want to. You know, I was in the IF once. I swore the oath of integrity and allegiance. My blood raced, my heart sang. I felt proud to live at that moment in history when standing armies had been replaced by an international force, a peace-making force, watching over the eradication of another age's weaponry.'

He wrenched a bottle from its optic as we passed the bar, tipped some down, grabbed my arm. We all stopped walking. He faced us.

'But it wasn't like that. The Force are just marking time, and they feel they've been marking it too long. What d'you think they do all the time? They move bits of hardware from place to place and pretend they're having little wars. They get fat and drunk, and every now and then things get a bit out of hand and they let one off. The research labs are a joke. A standing, roaring joke. So, I thought, what the eye doesn't see gives the heart no grief; this is as good a place as any for those that can't live with peace, here in a bit of the world where no one else has to see them, all the nasty left-overs together. When people said to me, hinting, heavy-lidded in their cups, "Spencer, our time will come, look at this, I got it from stores and I keep it under my pillow, want one?", I'd think, you dinosaur, you fool; and I made complaints about their attitude to people higher up. I was discharged. I was lucky. No one gets orders to wipe someone out. They think of it for themselves. They guess it. They're looking for the chance. But not everybody. Maybe you can be lucky too.'

The bartender's voice had shed its sharpness, its sprightly irony. 'But what the eye doesn't see gives all our hearts some grief.' He gestured around him. 'Oh yes, there's going to be another war, you'll live to see it, perhaps. . . .'

All three of us, our arms linked, walked on the shore as the sun went down and the bright contrasts of sea, sky and land crept gently closer together until everything was blue-grey, blue-black, black.

'It's hard to think of going back,' I said. 'I wanted to stay with the floating people, really, that's what I wanted to do.'

'But perhaps you can be a floating person anywhere,' the bartender said gently. 'You don't need water. You can read the signals and slip through gaps, you can work out a way to live in accordance with what you know.'

'That what you've done?' asked H.

The bartender stared him out. 'Yes,' he said.

We lit a fire on the beach.

'It might be tonight,' the bartender said, 'it might be tomorrow, but soon there'll be ships on the horizon. What are you two going to do?

'Now don't you worry about me. When I see them I'm straight to the Paradise bar and as many litres down the throat as I can stand to pour. After that I'm just a disposal problem like her in there – they won't get anything out of me, unless they've learned to revive the dead.

'There's life-jackets by the hundred in the store-room. Go off the north side and the currents'll take you straight into the shipping lines. Don't tell me you're afraid of drowning.'

H's face was carefully neutral.

'What did Jo do?' I asked him.

'Quality control in a processing lab. I could tell you – she had two years till retirement. But she could go early, being a mother. I know most of her numbers. Mine are just one digit more, you see. I could –'

'*Why did you take me with you?*' I'd said. 'Because you wanted to come so much,' he answered.

And now I saw wanting in the corners of his eyes: *take me back, you be Jo*. And I saw us at the beginning, seated round the table, when Jo was alive and she tossed her shining hair in the sun.

'All right,' I said. The decision came suddenly, like a bolt shooting home. It felt right, to have a kind of symmetry. And ever since I have been Jo, and clutched my own killer to my heart. Kept him safe, carried something for him, grown used to the weight. I've resolved something, kept it how it is.

The bartender was excited, hopping from foot to foot. 'Hide under the cloak of their concealment. Thick as mud, dark as ink, hard as steel,' he said, chuckling. 'Mind you, it's only a guess. But if it works, you'll know we were right, and that's something. I'll burn the overalls.'

So we left Island Paradise in orange life-jackets and, for verisimilitude, a few scraps of clothes the holiday-makers had left behind. As if my wish for the plane to crash into the sea had been fulfilled, and as mother and son. As if Jo had forgiven H, and he in turn had never fired that shot with perfect aim in the dark, through canvas and flesh and bone and brain. We left in the late afternoon. We donned our borrowed clothes and I remembered at the last minute the roll of film in my overalls pocket.

'Leave it,' said H, but I refused, wrapped it and pushed it carefully up my arse until I felt the skin close in a tight pucker behind it. The bartender rowed us out as far as he dared. We inflated the jackets and launched ourselves into the sea as if it was an enormous bath. Playfully, he pushed us away.

'Stay lucky,' he said, and we watched him row back into an Island Paradise sunset he would have loved and hated to describe, curdling it with the anger in his voice, the memory of other soured dreams.

We were sighted by a tanker after three days at sea. Our flesh was chapped and waterlogged, our eyes raw, our tongues were swollen and seemed to be growing into one skin with the roofs of our mouths and the backs of our throats. At first we literally could not speak and finding this made explanation less demanding, we pretended the condition continued much longer than it actually did. I wrote 'Island Paradise' and drew a simple sketch of an aeroplane plunging seawards; the captain and the doctor gasped. I drew two stick-figures floating in tumultuous seas and driving rain, I shrugged my shoulders, and H nodded gravely. We were put to bed like children, and slept in each other's arms. They were proud to have us with them, they said. . . . A mini-plane was chartered to pick us up.

Soon, we were flying through cloud, the brakes were on, the aerofoils tilted. The speeches were yet to come. I held H's hand, squeezing it tight as we broke through the cloud and saw below the patterns of our world, superimposed, syncopated. Cast over the land like nets were roads: inflows, outflows, ringways, freeways, radials and concentrics carrying their steady stream of vehicles, spaced even as heartbeats; beside them marched white armies of buildings that gathered into cities, stretched sparser along the outflows, beside which ran a straggling mesh of overland cables and pipes bearing Power, water, messages, effluent, to and from. Closer, and I saw the clutters of aerials and dishes, rooftop panels and launch pads, the sparkle of glass, the gathering of crowds and then, suddenly, a broad sweep of runways, roads to nowhere and places of no return. We were about to land; yet it seemed as if all we saw, this animated map, was impenetrable as deepest forest, hardest ice, and we would have to hack our way in. But already the seats pressed into our backs, and we were there.

'Welcome home.'

It's time to admit that I have regrets as well as grudges. I feel we missed our moment.

We stepped down to applause and we, the murderer and the disappeared, were on televideo, but we were called instead the *sole survivors* and bathed in camera light, blinding but protective. It was a terrible shame, we said, we had such a lovely time, right until the end.

We stood on the edge of the known world, all the travellers pausing on their journeys to see us, and that would have been our moment. The sky was heavy with imminent rain, white buildings rose on every side, the runways blinked with the clear colours that signal the systematic arrivals and departures of ordinary life. The airport staff were dressed in rocket-grey, the passengers on holiday flights wandered bemused between hope and disappointment, the mint-green tele-tables blinked news of time passing and to come, and, like the beat and roar of a surrounding sea, came the endless whirr of traffic, the televideos, the music.

We were glad to be alive, we said, as they filmed us arm in arm: that was our moment, we should have raised our fists above our heads and shouted, we should have killed each other then, mother and son, before the bedazzled toing and froing crowds, and everything we knew and were would have had its consummation and, perhaps, its consequences. Instead, we blinked like rabbits and clutched at each other's arms; we repeated our numbers; we feared discovery at any moment; overwhelmed by what we'd escaped from, we smiled our gratitude for being saved from the seas.

'Key in here,' someone said, placing in my hand a new identicard, still warm from the processor, on it an image of the me that had escaped, and embossed beneath that the name and number of a woman who died, Jo. Then my hand was gently guided towards the gate. I pushed the card into the slot. The scanner blinked and buzzed as it read. I looked at H; we were both scared. The gate opened. I waited the other side for him, faint with panic. He dropped his card, picked it up. The gate opened again. The bartender was right. And wrong.

*

We went to the toilets to escape the celebrations, which would have made the bartender laugh until he split his sides. The tiles and porcelain gleamed coldly. I felt claustrophobic. I ran the water as hard as it would go, imagining it overflowing the sink, filling the room. But only a thin trickle emerged, and the flow cut as soon as I took my hand away. Cautiously I looked in the mirror. It was nothing like the face I remembered. Fine lines sprang from the corners of my eyes and laced my forehead. From the cubicle, H said, 'What can we do now?' It sounded as if he was laughing.

'Nothing,' I said.

'Nothing,' he replied, imitating Speaker's grave tone.

The only thing I could think of would be to tell what had happened to other people. I imagined us approaching a stranger, together, like two people conducting a survey or selling something. *Excuse me. Have you got free time? There's something we'd like to tell you about. And some pictures to show you. It may take a little while.* I giggled. Impossible.

'Let's agree to forget it,' said H as we emerged.

We were famous. Next day we were on the announcements.

> In times of safety such as these, few experience what these two people have, mother and son tossed on the waves in heat and thirst and loneliness and, perhaps worst of all, uncertainty . . . their survival is a testimony to the characteristics of our age as embodied in its people: formidable health, a fierce optimism, and a profound ontological security. . . .

For a few weeks we lived the way all survivors do, as myths. We relocated, immediately, to avoid it being noticed that as I recovered from my ordeal I obviously grew less, rather than more, like the Jo people had known. And H began to call me Jo, even in private, saying it was simpler. For a year, he worked spasmodically with his camera, then stopped.

'I've lost the reason,' he said.

He works in the central registry of citizens, where people pass before him as codes without faces or stories.

'I want to keep things simple,' he says. 'Leave me alone, I can't be bothered.' He pins his hopes, as I thought I did, on our personal solution, killing – by – consent; he has held himself back for it so that nothing intervenes. In one way it is almost as if the H that drew me running across the golden sands of Island Paradise's longest beach has vanished as completely as the floating people did.

We talked tonight.

H! H, wake up. H, listen. It's what the bartender said.' He stared at me, his eyes heavy, and didn't reply, but I pushed on, I'm stronger now, despite the way I look: I feel better than I have for years.

'You can't have forgotten. Don't you see, it's happening now. Don't you see the announcements? It's like – it's a bit like what you tried to do – everything's going sky high –'

'No, it's not,' he said.

'I'm not satisfied,' I said.

'Not that stuff. I've heard all that somewhere before. What are you going to do then? Find the right door to knock on and walk through it with a bomb up your skirt? You won't live long enough to find the address. Come on, let's –'

'I'm not satisfied –'

'Shut up. Who d'you think you are? Let's –'

'No,' I said. 'H, listen. I won't do it. Never. I don't want to.'

'Jo –' began H, and reached blindly for me. To think,

I used to be afraid of what he might do. I never knew he had such tears, such wretched sounds inside him, gulps and whimpers, dry whispers, gasps, cracks, wails –

'Jo –'

'Don't call me Jo. I'm not Jo. I'm Laurie.'

'Please. Put all those photos away, why don't you? Jo – Laurie – I don't want it any more, what I wanted then . . . It's terrible – I wish I'd never . . .' I cradled him protectively '. . . never killed Jo.'

'So do I,' I said, folding the sheets about us as we sat on the edge of the bed, 'and lots of things.'

'But why,' I whispered when we had settled down, 'why did you do it? Why did you kill poor Jo? Don't just say you hated her. Why?'

He didn't push me away. His voice sounded hollow. 'To stop her being there.'

'But –' I moved closer '– she did no harm.' H began to shake.

'To stop me following her about. Because I could.' I waited.

'She never forgave me but she always said she did. She never would come but she always said she might. *I just might*.'

'But *I* did,' I said, gripping him hard. 'I came with you, H.' He struggled free and turned round so as to face me. The sheet twisted tight, binding us uncomfortably together.

'Yes,' he said. 'Laurie, don't go. I've got no real answer.'

'I've not forgiven you,' I said, touching his face in the dark, 'it's not my job, and she can't. You did it. And the other thing. The detonator in the cave.'

'You stopped me.'

'Yes,' our voices seemed to echo in the room.

'I knew you'd come.'

'That's a lie.' He didn't deny it. I shifted slightly, so that there was a space between us. He was still crying, I listened to him. This is my war, I thought, nearly fought and done.

'If we'd done it,' I said after a while, 'laid down by the light of the window – a suicide pact – if we'd done that and died, it would have been a kind of hiding, not an escape.'

'There isn't one,' said H.

Thirsty, we shared the last of my water. I slept before H. I drifted into a dream of lying in sunshine on a raft at sea. And then there was an explosion, but I was immune, and light streamed into a cave. I, Laurie, dreamed. I slept without thinking to check the locks.

Later, noise outside woke me up, and I in turn woke H and took him to watch with me at the window. We stood arm in arm. Two people were hitting each other close by one of the new memorials. One had a building block, the other a piece of twisted metal. It seemed to last for ever, they moved slower and slower, increasingly unsteady on their feet and inaccurate in their aim. There was no talking, just the soft thud of blows that met their target, the crash and scrape of those that didn't. In the building opposite the blinds were up, as if everyone there was watching too. The one with the building block fell to the ground, the one with the metal steadied himself, then knelt and put his ear to the other's chest. Surveillance didn't arrive until long after he'd disappeared; at the first whirr of propeller blades we watchers drew our blinds and went inside.

Last Days

H didn't go to work, and we saw it together this morning: the cave we once lived in. Starkly lit, the tarpaulins ripped back to expose the banks of equipment: more of it than I remember. A lingering close-up of the symbols of the rocket and the dove, crossed out. Here, we were told, the subversive agents hid out and attempted, by means of stolen equipment, to send their observations of Force's operations to the Enemy above. The waves broke, washed over black rock at the mouth of the cave where dolphins used sometimes to play. There was no sound on the film, but I heard the pulse of the sea, ssh-aah, as if I was there, and as the camera pulled away there was a glimpse of those careful outlines on the wall, one for each floating person that ever was, fitting exact.

> Give thanks that they were caught, but there may be others.

They must be dead. A finite life, finite lives, as they always were aware, but ending sooner, and closer together, than perhaps they thought. Leaving spaces on the wall. Or maybe they knew . . . and were they – were they even sending messages to –?

I looked at H and saw myself, tiny, in the pupils of his eyes. He pulled me close and whispered, 'You look *happy*.'

And need the floating people even be dead? Couldn't they have slipped through the net? After all, both H and I are on that wall, and we're still alive. And I realized there are two sides to not being able to believe what I hear and see on the announcements. One, that's kept me awake night after night: I don't know the truth; and the other: it could be better as well as worse, it could be anything.

Am I happy?

'Traitors!'

'Up the Enemy.'

Each day, the crowd stays longer in the square, shuffling and stamping and looking up at the sky, as if they'll be able to see the Enemy there, as if something will come hurtling down. The battle for Three has begun to disrupt life, it's taken people away from themselves. Not everyone shouts. Some engage each other in earnest speculation.

'It'd take three days to get there.'

'We're better off with Chemical –'

'The thing is, to destroy the Enemy without destroying Three . . .'

'But that means more people get killed, if we can't use the big stuff.'

Killed. Everyone says it now, it trips off the tongue.

'Depends whether they're on it, or somewhere outside, like us.'

'And if it was a question of stopping them from getting here, we'd have to consider it might be worth losing Three, even if the consequences . . .'

And some sit on benches, elbow on knee, hand on chin, and others stare still at the screen, as if expecting more information. Surveillance, now in their winter uniforms, are almost invisible in the snow. But if you come up close, their faces look anxious. They have been issued with megaphones, and after a while, though for no obvious reason, they'll begin to shout: please clear the square, please clear the square.

> As time passes, it is unfortunately possible that some people – a very few – will seek not to

improve what we have and to defend it against external threat, but to spoil it. They will say, thoughtlessly, because they can't remember and don't understand, 'Why don't we just turn everything upside down, try something else?' I submit that we must not be afraid of words, we must not be afraid to call these people enemies too, the enemies of peace.

Blue eyes is on every day now. His rhetoric soars as the Power-cuts worsen. People are sent home from work to sit in the early afternoon gloom. Vast amounts of data have been corrupted by sudden fluctuations. All over the world it's the same. There's talk of certain essential tasks having to be performed manually, by gangs of employees unable to do their usual work. Even when the light's on, it looks faint. This is what the Enemy does, blue eyes exhorts, do not despair.

'Blue eyes are blind,' I write on the marble white façade of Accounts Inc., not caring if I'm caught. The marker squeaks, its odour makes me faint, my fingers are cold, blue as eyes. Though my graffiti are always expunged, some others seem to escape. Little line-drawings and cartoons: figures with huge mouths and one eye or ten, or huge mechanical limbs, shot through with arrows, writhing in agony, flat on their backs. They make me laugh, and then I want to cry. For I can't imagine the Enemy's like any of these, we would have been shown it if it was. *Technical difficulties*. And if the Enemy came, in the night in the freezing dark, if we woke up in the morning and they were there – supposing, that is, they didn't think it was safer to eliminate us from a distance – what would it look like outside? Would we be able to see them? Would we know? How would they treat us?

I look about me in the square and watch everyone waiting for the same thing I'm waiting for. Our faces are thin and pinched, our breath swirls about us in the air, snow settles on our shoulders. Some say the severity of the winter is the Enemy's contrivance. We look like Time Before, waiting for deliverance. I look about me, I feel afraid, and sad, because suddenly I love the people in the square. I want to touch them and save them. Then I hate them and feel glad. Perhaps I am the Enemy. . . .

'What is it?' the Counsellor asked abruptly at the beginning of my last session. 'What is it that keeps you?'

'I'm not sure,' I stalled . . . 'I feel there's something I need to do.'

'Then it must be done,' she said. 'I'm here to help.'

Since her outburst, our conversations are brief and business-like. She won't tolerate silence, or diversions of any kind. She's pushing me.

'Go away and think about it. Tell me next week.'

'It's that I feel I need to make a journey,' I said to her this time, straight out. 'I need to go back to Island Paradise, just that.' I thought: today, we're going to strike a deal, that's what this is about. Like Briggs *et al.*

'You can't,' she said in an excessively patient tone, obviously infuriated by my naivety. 'As a retired person you're not entitled to holiday. And anyway, no one goes there any more.'

'Because of the –?'

'Because of over-use.'

'I think it would make *all the difference*,' I said.

She paused and considered, treating me to a steady, appraising stare. 'Why do you feel the need to make a journey?'

I hesitated, looked confused, as befits my condition. 'Afterwards, I think I'd be able to let go,' I replied.

Again, the stare. 'Would you say the accident and subsequent ordeal all those years ago impaired your perceptions or adjustment? The subsequent publicity and so on. Perhaps these events disrupted the pattern of your life, created desires nameless and unfulfillable, and fears that need to be assuaged? And would you say that a journey, say to the Golden Desert, would serve, so to speak, to readjust the balance and allow you to *let go*?'

Already her fingers were on the keyboard. She looked up. 'It's my job to help you find your Time. If you just want a free holiday, forget it,' she said.

'I'm sure it would help,' I said, gratefully. 'I think, you see, I'm afraid of another disaster. When I know it can't happen, then I'll be able to *let go*.'

She pressed request. The woman's a magician: Kim and I waited years for our turn to go to Paradise, but the Age Counsellor waited less than a minute for my answer.

'In the circumstances, it's allowed,' she said, handing me the vouchers and permits. 'Fifteen days in the Golden Desert. You can go next week. Take your son or a friend if you want. I've been there, it's wonderful. We had such a marvellous time. So good to get away. The landscapes are etched in my mind. . . . Mind you, I've heard it's not as pretty as it was,' she remarked. 'Something to do with climatic change. Perhaps I'll see you on your return.'

'Perhaps not,' I said suggestively, and she smiled, the first real one I've seen. She was satisfied: she thought I was another time-bomb skilfully unpicked, patiently interrupted, forestalled at the last moment without my knowing it; she thought I lay in quiet pieces that could be swept away. I was satisfied too, I shan't have to see her again. We shook hands.

Tonight we sat on opposite sides of our bed. The room was lit only by the yellowish light from lamps in the street below filtered through the thin mesh of the blinds and curtains, which puffed out then shrank back as if someone behind them was breathing softly.

'I want to be on the move. I've got tickets to the Golden Desert,' I said. 'I'm going in the morning; you can come if you want, it's up to you. . . .' For once it was absolutely quiet outside and the words had an unusual sharpness about them. I watched him. He looked very small, his face was drained of colour.

'I might,' he replied. 'What are you going to do?'

'I suppose it depends,' I said. 'Supposing you didn't come, I might have a couple of drinks in the bar, like last time. I'll be sitting in the aisle. The pilot will announce: "We're halfway to the Golden Desert, flying at so many thousand feet above the largest expanse of water on the planet." I'll look out and see it, deeps and shallows, the patches of weed and plankton in greens and greys and blues bleeding into each other under the perfect edge where water meets air; it'll be calm, the pattern of waves just a faint shimmer of light across its surface. Thin white clouds pass below the plane, and cast brief shadows over the water.

'I'll whisper to the steward: *Once there was a plane that never came back. It plunged into the sea on the way home and all but two, so the story goes, were drowned. I am one of those. I've come again because the thought of the disaster holds me back from Timely Death.* I'll show him my special ticket. *It's a mystery*, I'll say. *How it happened was never explained. I want to sit in the cockpit, I want to see the controls*, I'll say, *I want to see it's safe.*

'I'll sit quietly next to the pilot, a harmless old woman at the end of her time. I'll sit quietly for a while. Are you scared? he'll say. Oh no, I'll say. Is it difficult, flying? No, mostly automatic. Could I try? I'll say.

'We'll change places.'

H laughed, and I smiled before continuing.

'We'll change places,' I repeated. ' "This is the override, installed to cope with the unforeseen," he says. I play with it a little, letting us closer to the waves. "Gently," he says.'

'Ground control'll have something to say about that,' said H.

'"It's fine, just fine," I'll say, taking us all the time closer to the sea. "Island Paradise was the strangest place," I'll say, "people travelled so far to meet their dreams but when they got there they just turned back . . ." The water seems rougher now, waves rush over it like gooseflesh on a slack skin. "I didn't though –"'

'Surveillance'll have you in the hold by now,' said H.

I continue: '"I did something else –" "We're too low!" he shouts, reaching for my hand on the override. As I feel his hand closing over mine, I say: "Don't. I haven't finished. Don't, or I'll take her into the sea." We're that close, it looks like water now, not skin, and the swell of it could make you sick. "Tell them not to panic," I say. I pull the override a little further down against the pressure of his fist. I'm stronger than him because I want to be, because I'm pulling and he's pushing from the side. Because we're nearer to where I want to be than to where he wants to be. "Don't panic," the pilot announces. "Due to a temporary disruption we are flying at a very low altitude but there is no danger."

'"It was like this," I say. "The plane before was jammed because the controller wanted rid of the passengers who'd seen two murders and been covered in the dust of an illegal and unscheduled blast. There was nothing he could do."

'"What d'you want?" he asks.

'"Change course for the headquarters of the International Council," I say –'

'Control would rather let you plunge into the sea, or send the Force to get you down. They won't care. That hijack stuff hasn't worked since before the Unfought War,' said H.

I answered, 'OK. This is what happens. There's spray in the air, it's splattering on the windows, drying white. We are travelling at two thousand kilometres an hour only twenty metres above the sea. The sea's invisible; all we see is a white streaking of speed. The passengers are terrified; they disobey the stewards, they push past the

Surveillance officer, also terrified; the fastest of them burst into the flight cabin. The others crush behind. "Don't panic, don't panic," the pilot shouts unasked. "Panic all you like," I yell. "We're going into the sea. Island Paradise is poisoned, weapons are hurtling in the sky. Briggs, Minito, Ellulah and Karanchek lied. You dream of killing, everyone does, everyone knows there's going to be a war. Wake up, panic."

'They lunge towards me. The plane swoops up, plummets down. The pilot's speaking to Control: "Take over, take over! There's a woman. She wants to fly to the Council headquarters and make accusations; she says she wants to knock on someone's door."

'Water hits the screen in hurled handfuls. The peaks of the strongest waves strike the underside of the plane. I let go of the override. Some of the passengers are pushing it up, others are pulling down. The plane's systems fumble and falter, can't obey such rapidly alternating instructions. I lean back and let the people clamber over me. The pilot repeating his message "she wants a confrontation –" is pushed aside.'

H was silent.

'The moment before Control could have taken over, we slice into the sea. The engine cuts. The lights go out, we're in a green underwater glow that's growing dimmer. Water enters through the exhaust. The plane fills with steam which condenses instantly on every surface, even our faces and hair. We hear metal cracking and a series of small explosions. We travel on, under our own momentum, but slowing against the water's resistance. Everyone falls silent, watching the first trickle of water seeping from under the window seal and running in a thin sheet down the inside of the glass.

'"I wanted this to happen," a woman says. Her eyes are sunken, her hair's tangled, her holiday dress blotched with sweat. She's looking at me, amazed. The passengers move apart a little. They begin talking quietly with each other. They are asking each other questions. Their eyes light up, they do not notice the thinning of the air, the growing pressure. The plane fills with voices and water together.' H and I are sitting on the bed. Outside a siren wails.

'It's only a guess,' I say, 'will you come?'

'Why not,' he says, 'take the plane up, instead of down?'

'Why not? Anything you like. We could go and meet the Enemy!' There's a long silence. 'I'd like to dream of elsewhere,' I say, 'an elsewhere without having to go away. A really different kind of end, with no dying in it. People in the street, led by us old, our grey and white hair streaming in the wind. A new start, with no Price to pay except there being no hiding place. Surveillance tearing off their uniforms. . . .' The muscles in my neck were growing tight, like a fist; my eyes ached. 'Elsewhere, somewhere where no one died, but I can't.'

I didn't want to cry. I cleared my throat and told him, 'H, I am actually dying. Really.' I showed him the evidence; the lumps and bumps, the enlarging patch of skin, stretching now from chest to neck, that seems almost transluscent. He touched it carefully. I described the other symptoms, the sense of my heart missing every other beat for minutes on end, the roaring in my ears. 'But there's no pain, I don't know why.'

I opened the desk drawer and took out the photographs of Jo, my papers and all the other rubbish, and put them in the middle of the floor.

'What –'

'Everything,' I said. Silently, he helped me gather all my possessions together, and then, unasked, fetched his to include in the pile. We added the collection of unused appliances, the oven, and such of the light fittings and so on as we could easily remove. He looked at me expectantly.

'Stand by the wall,' I said, pushing his shoulders back against it, lifting his arms from his sides and spreading the fingers out flat on the wall. 'Don't move.' Carefully, I chalked round his shape, keeping the line close.

'Where shall I put you then?' he said.

'Opposite.' I closed my eyes and felt his fingers pushing through my clothes to find my true edge. I listened to his breathing, held now and then in concentration.

'There.' He dusted his fingers; the dry sound in the dark made me almost see them: small, in a fist, open, tying rope.

We covered our pile of possessions in a sheet, then went out in search of some fuel or solvent to set them on fire; we didn't want to leave anything behind. But it's impossible to obtain these days; we abandoned the effort. Carrying only our special tickets to the Golden Desert, we walked for hours round the intermittently lit and freezing city. We held hands. Now and then we stopped outside a Residential like ours, and listened, to see if anyone else was awake. But the sounds I thought I heard always seemed to come from somewhere else. And we paused, stamping to keep warm, in public squares, where the telescreen loomed silent, and we looked, heads back, up at the sky. The cold and absence of lighting made the stars seem unusually bright, shimmering like liquid, and somehow closer.

'Perhaps they are falling back,' I said.

'What?'

'The missiles from the Unfought War. The ones they diverted into space, all that time ago. Perhaps they are falling back.'

'I used to think that too,' said H, 'when I was small.'

'You still are,' I joked.

'Compared to what?'

These could be our last words, I thought, as we strained against each other, trying to be the taller one.

Just before dawn it became colder than we could stand, and we returned to the flat with its pile of possessions and drawings on the wall.

‘I’ll come, of course,’ he said, just before I slept, ‘wherever, and do what you want.’

We’re still here. But here is a different place. This morning that awful noise summoned us to the square. There is a new president. He looks even younger than blue eyes, who died yesterday. They didn’t bother to say Untimely or not. He just died. The new one has freckles. A boy king. And now, officially, he declared in a steady but rather high voice, ‘We are at war.’

A great wave of noise rose and towered above us, whoops and wails chanting, screams, claxons, breaking glass. And someone even began heaving stones at the telescreen, but it wouldn’t break and freckle-face still spoke; he looked desperate, he was shouting, but I couldn’t hear through the noise of the crowd; he had his eyes screwed shut and he was shouting the same thing time and time again – and then the picture was gone. Perhaps he was telling the truth, or a bit of it, four or five words’ worth, lost. The noise grew louder. Surveillance advanced, speaking through their megaphones: ‘Clear the square’ – a faint whisper that few heard above the rising din. Their right hands were in their pockets. H and I turned to each other.

‘I’m afraid,’ we said together.

Some of the crowd began to run, desperate, fleeing senselessly at first, and then I saw her again, the big old woman I thought was Martina, capless, her grey hair streaming out behind her as she ran, her cheeks flushed, her arms raised above her head; she was shouting, roaring. People were following. Eagerly, H pulled at my arm.

‘Look! Shall we –?’ His face was alight. I took a step forward, and it seemed that something inside me burst, my insides were tearing, and I fell.

*

H carried me home. I'm on the floor, next to the pile we made. He's writing for me. The whisper of his sleeve brushing over the page, close by. I can't see. I can hear sounds from outside, never heard such noise. I shan't ask him to look. I don't want to know, not any more.